KILLER'S LAUGHTER

The telegram was a peel of triumphant laughter from a successful killer. It rang the death knell for an old man whose grandson was one of the victims. It brought home the horror of murder to Marion Loring and set her wondering about her nearest and dearest.

Somebody was responsible — and there was a great inheritance involved. There were further shocks in store for Marion after the two deaths in her family, when she found that police attention was firmly fixed on her. But Superintendent Beech, assisted by Inspector Morton, must investigate this case fully.

KILLER'S LAUGHTER

Isobel Lambot

First published 1968
by
Robert Hale Ltd

This edition 2002 by Chivers Press
published by arrangement with
the author's estate

ISBN 0 7540 8617 8

British Library Cataloguing in Publication Data available

Printed and bound in Great Britain by
Bookcraft, Midsomer Norton, Somerset

CHAPTER 1

THERE was no sound in the room but the laboured breathing of the dying man. Marion Loring listened to it, pressing her hot forehead against the cool windowpane, seeing and not seeing the view of rolling country, the scatter of tall trees, and the flash of sunlight on the tip of the lake.

"Murder. It's murder, as surely as if he had been stabbed."

An answering, sympathetic cough from the other side of the room told her that she had spoken the thought aloud.

She turned away from the window.

The room was large, darkish from the ancient panelling, although two mullioned windows let in the clear summer light. The great bed was in shadow, the heavy curtains bunched at the corners half screening the occupant. Patches of sunshine lay on the polished oak of the floor, touching fire from the colours of the rugs.

There was a movement from the far side of the bed, the soft sound of a chair scraping back, as the doctor left his place beside his patient. He came round the massive four-poster, walking quietly out of habit. Not that any footsteps would bring Robert Winter out of the sleep which was setting him upon his last journey.

The doctor was a thick-set man, tall, broad-shouldered, clad in the tweeds which are almost a uniform in the country. Passing through a shaft of sunlight, his greying red hair shone suddenly with its old gleam. It occurred to Marion, watching him, that this kindly, jovial man, whom she had known all her life, was ageing. She wondered why she should suddenly notice it now. On reflection, it was a process which had been going on for some time. Ever since his wife had died, three years ago. Perhaps if Mrs Ludlow were still alive. . . .

Geoffrey Ludlow had reached the girl's side. He looked down into her pale face and thought that she was taking it hard. Pity. Marion was a pretty little thing. He had brought her into the world, in the big old room in the rambling Vicarage down in the village. A long time ago. He had been young himself then, and conceitedly telling his father that he was old-fashioned.

"How old are you, Marion?" he asked abruptly.

"Twenty-two." She made no effort to hide her surprise.

He sighed.

"Time goes on so."

He needed no reminder of what Time brought : age and death. Both were present in the room, in the person of the man in the bed. And young Marion was seeing the stable world of her childhood disintegrate around her.

"It won't be much longer," he told her gently. "He may last another couple of days. Or it may be only a matter of hours."

Marion bent her head, and the soft fair hair fell forward, hiding her face from him.

"He's not suffering," Ludlow added.

The girl's head came up.

"It's not right, that anyone should do this to him," she said angrily.

Dr Ludlow wondered why he had ever thought of her as insipid. Probably because he had a preference for dark women. Roused, with that proud tilt of her head, and those blue eyes stormy, Marion Loring was worth more than a second glance from any man. So there was spirit there, after all, under the quiet exterior.

Spirit and what else? he asked himself, curious.

"It must be the same person who killed James and Alice," she went on, "Nothing else makes sense."

Ludlow felt a spurt of irritation. He had always considered James Winter a fool. The man being dead didn't alter the fact, but Ludlow felt ashamed for his opinion.

"Does any of it make sense?" he demanded, roughly.

Marion shook her head.

"Not to me. Perhaps the police . . ." her voice trailed into silence, as she glanced back to the bed.

"There is nothing more that we can do for him," Ludlow said in her ear, "Only wait."

Marion went across to the bed and stood looking down at the dying body. The old man's face was peaceful; it might have been an ordinary sleep but for the unnaturally heavy breathing. She knew that he would never wake, never open those shrewd eyes again. And all of this had been intended. . . .

She felt the anger boil up inside her.

There was a gentle tap at the door, then, immediately, without waiting for an answer, it opened and a neat dark head appeared round it.

"There's a call for you, Doctor. From your surgery."

Ludlow moved forward.

"Thank you, Mrs Lightfoot." He glanced at Marion. "I'll have to go."

She nodded.

"We can manage."

"Let me know if there is any change."

Then he was gone, but she was still not alone. The housekeeper who had summoned him away, had slipped into the room.

"That policeman's here," she announced.

Marion looked up eagerly.

"What does he say?"

Mrs Lightfoot shrugged.

"Nothing. You know that. Just asks questions. As if we could tell him anything."

She was a big woman, heavy but not fat, who had an unfailing ability to make Marion feel that she was a little girl again. Not that Mrs Lightfoot could look back to the time when a lonely little orphan of ten had made the journey from the village up to the house on the hill to make her home with her godfather. Grace Lightfoot had come to Astonley a mere four years ago, yet she exuded the aura of an old retainer.

There was an antagonism towards the girl in her every movement, as though she resented her as an interloper. Marion felt it now, jarring on her senses in this place of death.

"I don't suppose that Inspector Morton will want to see me again," she said quietly, "I'll sit with him for a bit. Tell Nora, will you?"

Mrs Lightfoot sniffed.

"That one has gone down into the village, to the Post Office."

She made it sound like a major crime.

Marion sat down in the chair by the bed.

"I'll be all right. I'll ring if I need any help. Or if there is any change," she added, her eyes on the beloved face of the man whom she had always called Uncle Robert, although there was no blood tie between them.

Mrs Lightfoot lingered for a moment, gazing down broodingly at her employer, then sniffed loudly once more, and took herself off.

In the quiet room, Marion sat, listening to the laboured breathing, and wondering what they had done to be plunged into this nightmare.

There was another interruption. A soft knocking at the door and a murmured inquiry brought a visitor. The new arrival was an elderly man, rotund and puffing slightly from the climb up the staircase.

Marion stood up and put out her hands to him. He came to the bedside and took them, pressing them between his own.

"Well, my dear?" he asked gently.

Marion felt the tears welling up in her eyes. Somehow the anger had ebbed away and she was left forlorn in the desert at the end of the world.

"Oh, Sir John," she gulped, "he's dying."

She pulled her hands away and groped for a handkerchief.

Sir John Prout made no movement to stop her. Let the child cry, he thought; she must, or she won't be able to bear what is bound to come.

He stood looking down at his old friend in the bed. A good chunk of his own life was bound up with Robert Winter, and when he was gone, the gap would not be filled. And he found himself remembering, with vivid clarity, how the two of them had fought, here in this very garden at Astonley, over some girl or other. He couldn't even recall her name now, but they had both fancied themselves in love with her. One had lost a tooth and the other gained a black eye in her service that day. And then she had upped and married some other fellow.

Half a century ago.

Robert Winter began to make loud gasping noises.

Sir John glanced at the girl.

"Better call someone, Marion."

She nodded, dumbly, and stumbled over to the bellpush beside the bed.

Within minutes, it seemed that the room was full of people. Mrs Lightfoot arrived and on her heels, a smart blonde woman, who immediately took charge of the sick-room. She began bustling about by the bed, shooing the others away. Marion, leaning against the wardrobe for support, sickeningly sure that the awaited moment had arrived, was aware that more people had entered the room, but she did not bother to look at them. Her attention was fixed on the bed.

The blonde woman said sharply, "I think it would be better if you all went out of the room. Mrs Lightfoot, will you please get Dr Ludlow back at once." The housekeeper disappeared quickly. "Now, if you don't mind," the blonde continued, "I'll call you when it is necessary."

Marion did not move. She felt that her legs would not carry her even as far as the corridor, although she knew that Nora was right to drive them all out. She was Uncle Robert's nurse and she knew what had to be done.

Someone made a murmured protest, and Nora's voice came again.

"I'm sorry, Mrs Winter, but I really must have everyone outside for a little while."

Marion realised that Aunt Rosalie was there and was trying to make a nuisance of herself. Then someone took her arm and began to lead her to the door. She went without a word, stumbling in the wake of the others, held up by the strong hand under her elbow.

The bedroom door shut firmly behind them. They grouped like wandering sheep in the dark passage outside.

"My dear Rosalie," Marion heard Sir John's voice, some way ahead of her, "The girl is only doing her job. Let's hope Ludlow hasn't gone too far away. These changes take place. It may not be the end."

Marion felt the hold on her arm tighten, and she looked round at her supporter, whose face gleamed dimly white in the gloom.

David.

Naturally.

David was one of those people who was usually at hand when needed.

"I hope to God it is the end," he muttered, "There's no hope. I can't bear this waiting around."

Marion was vaguely shocked. If it had been anyone but David she would have thought them callous.

Ahead of her, Rosalie Winter was still complaining, but they were moving now, out of the short dark passage into the bright light from the great windows of the hall. Across the minstrels' gallery and down the wide sweep of the oak staircase. Through the hall at the bottom and into the drawingroom, by common unspoken consent, all keeping together.

Mrs Lightfoot met them at the drawingroom door.

"The doctor is on his way. He will be here in a few minutes."

Rosalie, her composure re-established, nodded.

"Thank you. I think we could do with some coffee, Mrs Lightfoot, please."

For a moment, it seemed as if the housekeeper would dispute the command. Then she gave one of her eloquent sniffs and stalked off in the direction of the kitchen.

One of the group detached himself from the others and hurried after her, dropping a cheerful wink at Marion as he passed her.

In spite of herself, Marion had to smile back at him. But that was Roderick all over, making one smile at a time like this. And no doubt he was out to smooth down Mrs Lightfoot too, and cajole her into making coffee to please him rather than at his mother's command.

All the same, it was a bit heartless when his grandfather lay dying.

Murdered.

David pushed her gently into the drawingroom, where Rosalie and Sir John were already seated, and making some sort of conversation.

Marion looked up at him. He was quite unlike the rest of the family, although there was a blood connection. Fair and squarely built, he took after some other line, perhaps his mother's, who had lived in this part of the country for centuries longer than the Winters or any others, until imprudent finance had scattered the young ones to earn their keep where they could. Which had brought him to his distant cousin's estate as land agent.

Now the usually open features were clouded.

"There's a chap waiting for me in the office," he said abruptly, "I'll have to deal with him. Rosalie, let me knew if—anything happens."

He went out without another word or glance at Marion.

Rosalie Winter scarcely noticed that he had gone. She had dropped her pretence at conversation with Sir John, and was staring vacantly out of the window at the other side of the room. She was a good-looking woman, slender and without a trace of grey in the shining black hair. It was difficult to recall that she had grown children. As usual, she was impeccably dressed.

Outside there was the sound of a car, then hurried footsteps crossing the hall and clattering on the bare wood of the stairs.

"Ludlow," muttered Sir John, unable to resist the temptation to rise and wander out into the hall.

Rosalie and Marion followed him.

Mrs Lightfoot was coming from the kitchen, a tray in her hands. Behind her came Roderick, dark and slender as his mother, with still a lurking mischief in his pointed face.

At that moment, Nora Deeping appeared at the end of the minstrels' gallery.

She singled out Rosalie.

"Will you come up, Mrs Winter? Mr Roderick, too."

They all went, trailing after old Robert Winter's daughter-in-law and his grandson. Rosalie and Roderick passed into the bedroom.

A long five minutes later, the door opened again. Dr Ludlow, his face grave, looked out.

"You can all come in now."

But no one moved.

"Is he—gone?" asked Sir John quietly.

Geoffrey Ludlow nodded.

"Yes."

He stood aside for them to enter. The room was unnaturally quiet now that the heavy breathing had ceased. They stood in a cluster at the foot of the bed. Then Nora gently drew the sheet over the dead face.

Marion felt a hand on her arm, but not a support in trouble. More like a vice. She tried to move away but the fingers tightened cruelly.

"He's dead," rasped a voice, which she hardly recognised as belonging to Grace Lightfoot, "He's dead. And I hope you are satisfied, Marion Loring."

CHAPTER 2

Sir John Prout was thankful that he could say truthfully that he expected the imminent arrival of visitors at his house, and so make his escape from Astonley. Never had he been more glad to leave the place. He drove away without a glance to right or left, leaving the great gabled West Front mellow in the sunshine and the gardens a blaze of colour all round. Sir John cared nothing for the sight. All he wanted was to get away.

He turned out of the huge gates and into the road leading down into the village of Winsmere. Normally he loved the drive, for all its familiarity. It was always a joy to him to roll slowly down the hill from the gates of Astonley, and see spread before him the lake, and beside it, the ancient church, and the cluster of time-worn roofs and cottage gardens. But today he was oblivious to the patterns of the hedgerows, to the gentle sweep of the road, even to the stretch of water from which the village took its name.

He was through the village and up the narrow lane leading to his own home before he realised it.

He was thinking that the situation at Astonley was potentially a very nasty one. Not that Rosalie hadn't handled it well. Much better than he would have expected. She must be made of sterner stuff than he had supposed. And Dr Ludlow, too, had surprised him. Remarkably quick on the uptake. Between them, he and Rosalie had cleared poor old Robert's bedroom in a jiffy, neatly separating the warring parties.

Not that anyone could hope to keep the lid down on that sort of thing indefinitely. Particularly with the police in the house. And it wouldn't do any good packing that poisonous Lightfoot woman off. She'd spread her tale, regardless, and getting rid of her might only make bad worse.

And, the Lord knew, people would listen to her. Bound to, in a case of murder.

Though how anyone who knew her could suspect Marion Loring of engineering her godfather's death was beyond him.

But Sir John had lived on this earth for the best part of eighty years and he knew that people would believe anything. Young Marion was in for a sticky time.

The only hope was that the police would lay hold of the true culprit quickly.

If they could.

A gust of anger blew through him at the enormity of the whole thing. He had never experienced anything like it. True enough, people in these parts were no angels. Murders happened now and again. But normal murders : a blow in anger to stop a nagging tongue, or a drunken brawl. Nothing—like this.

There was a car parked in front of the neat Georgian façade of his home. Seeing it, Sir John growled to himself. He was late. His guests had arrived to find him absent.

The front door of the house opened and a girl in a cotton frock ran out, waving to him. Seeing her, Sir John felt some of the burden lift from him. She was by far his favourite grandchild, and at this moment, with a light breeze lifting her short brown curls, so much like her dear, dead grandmother when he had gone courting her, that his heart turned over. It was hard for him to remember that she was a successful professional woman and, for the past few months, a wife. He was ashamed at the little spurt of jealousy which the recollection brought in him.

He climbed stiffly out of the car.

"Hope, my dear! Have you been here long?"

She embraced him briefly, joyfully.

"Only ten minutes, Grandpa."

"You're looking radiant," he said simply, staring at her, "Marriage agrees with you."

Hope Warren laughed.

"Charles hasn't started beating me yet. Here he is."

A tall dark man had appeared at the open front door.

"How are you, sir? I'm sorry we are so early. Hope insisted leaving Town at the crack of dawn."

"Not a bit. I said to be here in time for lunch. My fault I wasn't here when you arrived. I was over at Astonley."

Hope's face clouded over.

"Poor Mr Winter! We read about James and his wife, of course. How is he taking it?"

Sir John led them into the house.

"Robert's dead."

"Oh, no!"

The old man tramped on steadily ahead of them.

"Let's have some sherry. I'll tell you about it."

He was thinking: I'm glad they are here; I need to talk about it; and to someone who could not possibly be involved.

Behind him, the Warrens exchanged glances. They followed him in silence into his comfortable little study.

Sir John brought out a bottle and glasses. As he poured, another thought occurred to him. It might not be a bad idea to interest Charles Warren in the case. Of course, the police might solve the whole thing quickly. But, on the other hand, they might not. As far as he knew they had made no headway over the deaths of James and Alice. And Marion might need special help. He searched round in his mind for an approach.

Hope gave it to him.

"What did Mr Winter die of, Grandpa?"

"A stroke."

Her face cleared.

"Oh, well, then. He'd had one before, hadn't he?"

Sir John nodded.

"Last year."

Charles Warren's eyes had narrowed.

"But what brought on the stroke?" he asked quietly, and Sir John shot him a grateful look for so quick a perception.

Hope looked merely puzzled.

"But, Charles, any shock can do it. Surely you know that."

Charles grinned at her.

"Yes, my dear Doctor, I do."

Hope pulled a face at him.

"I should have thought that the shock of the double murder of his eldest grandson and wife would have been enough to bring on another stroke."

Charles shook his head.

"I don't think that is quite the point, is it, Sir John?"

Hope frowned.

"I don't follow. What have I missed that you have noticed?"

"The time factor. I wouldn't dispute with you on medical matters. That's your job. But if the stroke were to be brought on by the news of the double murder, wouldn't you expect it to happen more or less immediately?"

"Yes, I would. Certainly within a day or so. You mean, this one wasn't? Charles, how can you know?"

"Because your grandfather would have written and told us. We had a letter from him three days ago, and there was no mention of Mr Winter." He turned to his host. "Am I right, sir?"

"You are," Sir John replied heavily.

"And James and his wife died a fortnight ago."

"He took it remarkably well, all things considered," Sir John said suddenly, "He had this last stroke yesterday."

"Then it was a perfectly normal one," said Hope firmly. "How old was he?"

"Eighty-one. But it wasn't a normal course of events, Hope. It was murder. Deliberate, premeditated murder."

"But how?" she demanded.

"It was a telegram," Sir John replied, surprisingly, "Yesterday morning, Robert received a telegram. Marion took it in to him, unopened. He opened it, read it—and that was that. He never regained consciousness. He died this morning, while I was over there."

"And what was the text of the telegram?" Charles inquired.

But Sir John shook his head.

"I can't tell you. I haven't seen it. No one has, except Dr Ludlow. Robert had it in his hand when the stroke took him. They couldn't prize it loose. When the grip relaxed, Ludlow shot straight off to the police with it. But I gather that it was from the chap who wrote the letter and who presumably killed James and Alice Winter."

Into the silence which followed these words, there came the sharp ringing of the front door bell, and then the steps of someone from the back of the house passing down the flagged hall to answer it.

"I wonder—" Sir John began, and stopped, listening to the murmur of voices, one female, one male.

He flung open the study door and looked out into the hall.

"Oh, it's you, Inspector," he said, "Please come in." He glanced back into the room. "Police," he informed his guests.

"We can make ourselves scarce," Hope offered, looking at her husband, who made no sign of moving from his chair.

"No, no," her grandfather said quickly. "Charles might

find it interesting. Mightn't you, Charles?"

The note of appeal was unmistakable.

Charles Warren hid a smile. He had realised some minutes ago that the old boy had a purpose in telling him the story.

"I'm interested," he agreed.

It was the simple truth.

Sir John looked gratified.

"In here, Inspector," he called.

A firm tread was heard in the hall.

"We're in the study," Sir John went on, "Inspector Morton, isn't it?"

"That's right, sir," said a voice outside the door.

Sir John stood aside to usher in the visitor. The Inspector was a large, fair man in a dark suit. He stopped abruptly when he saw the Warrens.

"Well, here's a surprise and no mistake," he exclaimed, "What are you doing here, Mr Warren? Don't tell me we've got a bunch of spies in Winsmere?" He glanced at Hope. "And Dr Simister, too. I had an idea you two would stick together. I suppose it's Mrs Warren now?"

"It is," Hope told him, laughing.

"I'm not here on business, Inspector," Charles assured him. "Purely social. Visiting my wife's grandfather."

"Do you know each other?" demanded Sir John, at the first moment that he could get in a word.

"We met in Crowbury last year," Charles told him.

"I see," murmured Sir John wistfully.

No one seemed inclined to amplify the statement. As an explanation, it fell far short of Sir John's wishes. He knew that there had been a nasty incident, involving a couple of murders in the village of Crowbury, some thirty miles away, where his daughter and her family lived. And Charles Warren had been involved. But everyone had been maddeningly reticent about it all. And Charles himself was a bit of a mystery. Some high official in the Ministry of Security, whatever that might be. Counter-intelligence, Sir John supposed. He had been hoping that, on this their first visit to him since their marriage, he might manage to winkle some of the truth of the Crowbury affair out of them. But now with all this excitement here. . . .

All the same, it could be useful that Charles knew Inspector Morton, apparently quite well.

The Inspector was looking at Charles thoughtfully.

"This is a damned queer affair, if you like," he said.

"I was just telling them about it," Sir John broke in, "But, of course, I can't pretend to know the whole thing."

Morton was surprised into a laugh.

"But I do, sir? Is that it?"

Charles Warren looked up.

"I'll admit I'm curious. I hardly know a thing about it. Sir John had only just begun to tell me."

"Sit down, Inspector." Sir John pushed a chair towards the man.

Morton did as he was bidden. In a way, he wasn't sorry to see Charles Warren. He was confident that they would get to the bottom of the thing eventually, and he hoped that the day would never dawn when he had to ask for help outside the police force. But he had learned a great respect for Warren and for that boss of his, Liston. It wouldn't hurt to interest them in this. And they had channels of information which were closed to him. It was early days yet, but he had a nasty feeling that he was going to need all the help that he could get.

"I'll fill you in, then," he said, coming to a decision, "Briefly, the facts are these. Six weeks ago, there was a call to the Regional Crime Squad—to me, in fact—to come over here to see Mr Robert Winter. He had received an anonymous letter. It turned out to be the usual sort of thing. Newsprint stuck on a sheet of plain paper, to form a message. This one was a threat of murder. But not to Mr Winter himself. The person threatened was his son, Mr James Winter."

"Odd," Charles commented, "Why not to James himself?"

"I don't know. My guess is that it was to upset the old man, whose health wasn't all that good after the stroke he had a year ago. Anyway, he passed the matter over to us. And we found—nothing. The postmark was a London one. It had been posted in the City. The words had been cut from a London evening newspaper. And that was all we did find. We warned James Winter to watch out for himself and offered to keep an eye on him for a while. He laughed at us."

"You never could tell James anything," Sir John muttered.

"But didn't you have any idea who might have sent the letter?" asked Hope. "Had Mr Winter any enemies? He must have had."

Morton sighed.

"We checked. The only lead we could come up with was a fellow who had been sacked from Astonley, and who had gone off muttering that Mr Winter would be sorry for it. Not that we could find him in the London area. He could have been around, though, for all we knew. So much for the letter. After a month, nothing had happened, and we began to think it must have been a hoax."

"But it wasn't," murmured Charles. "What happened to James? I read a bit about it in the paper. He was living in Hampstead, wasn't he?"

"Yes. In a place where people come and go all the time and no one notices anything. This brings us to a fortnight ago. James's house was burgled. It wasn't done particularly well. The intruder knew enough to wear gloves, but otherwise it looked like the work of an amateur. That was the opinion of the local police. And in a way they were right. Some silver was pinched, which was found later by a gang of kids, in a ditch on the Heath. It's clear to us now that the burglary was a blind. This chap wasn't interested in the silver. All he wanted was an opportunity to stir a good load of arsenic into a dish of stewed fruit in the refrigerator."

"Goodness!" exclaimed Hope inadequately.

Morton smiled ruefully.

"James Winter and his wife Alice ate it the next day. There was enough in it to kill a dozen. They hadn't a chance. Of course, we stepped up the hunt for the fellow who had been sacked. We found him all right. In Walton Jail, where he had been for a couple of months. I suppose he was bound to end up in prison sooner or later, but it stood him in good stead this time. One hell of a good alibi. Not that I would bother with him now," Morton went on softly, "This thing comes much nearer home. I reckon the murderer hoped the shock of James's death would finish off his grandfather. And that means that not only was he well-acquainted with the state of Mr Winter's health, but also that he had means of finding out if the shock had induced another stroke. But it didn't. So he had to resort to other methods."

"The telegram," said Charles.

Morton felt in his pocket and pulled out his notebook. From it, he extracted a small piece of paper.

"Here's a photostat of it."

Charles took the paper. Hope and Sir John peered over his shoulder to read it.

"Nasty, isn't it?" Morton commented.

It read:

"YOU SHOULD HAVE BELIEVED MY LETTER STOP I SAID I WOULD AND I HAVE STOP I AM LAUGHING"

CHAPTER 3

An uneasy peace had fallen over Astonley. But it was only a waiting quiet. Troubles would descend on them soon enough.

Sunlight filtered in through the ancient glass of the drawingroom windows. It touched the fair bowed head of Marion Loring where she sat on a low chair near the fireplace. There was no fire now, in the heat of the summer, and the empty grate was filled with a large vase of bright flowers. Marion stared blindly at them.

From the depths of the wing chair opposite—Robert Winter's favourite chair—Rosalie Winter watched her.

"Don't take it to heart, Marion," she said suddenly, "The poor woman was hysterical."

From the other side of the room, Roderick laughed. Rosalie frowned at her son.

"Come off it, Mother," he said, unabashed, "Females like the Lightfoot don't go into hysterics. Do they, Geoffrey?" he added, appealing to Dr Ludlow, who had just appeared in the open doorway.

"Do they what?" he parried.

"Have hysterics."

Dr Ludlow looked as though he wished that he were elsewhere. He advanced into the room reluctantly.

"No, she's not the hysterical type," he agreed heavily.

Rosalie made a small eloquent movement of protest, of rejection.

Ludlow shook his head.

"I'm sorry, Rosalie. You'll have to accept that. I'm afraid all that was quite deliberate."

"Where is she now?" asked Rosalie wearily.

"In her sittingroom. Nurse Deeping is with her. Not that she can do anything. But they both have to be somewhere, and at least she can keep an eye on Mrs Lightfoot for us."

"The point is," Roderick chipped in, "that we must decide what to do about her."

"What *can* we do?" his mother almost snapped at him. "We can't sack her and send her away, much as I would like to. I have never cared for her, but I have to admit that she is an excellent housekeeper. The whole thing is out of our hands at the moment. Apart from how it would look if we got rid of her, Inspector Morton informed me this morning that he expects us all to stay put for the time being."

Marion looked up.

"Would it be better if I went? I'm sure Sir John would let me stay with him for a little while. That wouldn't upset the police." A thought struck her. "Unless Sir John wouldn't care to have Inspector Morton hanging round the place."

"My dear child," Rosalie replied briskly. "Being morbid about it won't help in the least."

"But he is bound to come after me, Aunt. After what Mrs Lightfoot said. She will be sure to tell him, too."

"She's right, Mother," Roderick chimed in, impishly, "And they could make out a bit of a case, you know. After all, Marion was Grandpa's secretary. You would have expected her to open telegrams for him. But she gave him that one, unopened."

"Roderick!" Rosalie exclaimed, scandalised, "That is quite enough of that. Anyone would think that you believed that frightful Lightfoot woman."

Roderick was unrepentant.

"I was only trying to open Marion's eyes—and yours, too, Mother—to the danger. The police will listen to the Lightfoot just as they will listen to us. And they will make up their own minds whom to believe."

"You don't have to spell it out to me, Rod," said Marion, "You know why I gave him that telegram unopened. It's the truth, even if no one will believe me. I know quite well that people could put a wrong construction on it. Do you think that I'm not blaming myself for giving him the thing unopened?"

"Marion, don't!" Rosalie broke in, "We believe you, and there is no reason why the police should not. They are not fools. They will get Mrs Lightfoot's measure quickly enough. And there is absolutely no question of your moving out. If you feel that you can't live under the same roof as Mrs Lightfoot, we will fix her up at the pub in the village. And let her talk her head off. She will anyway."

Marion jumped up.

"Please, no. I can put up with it."

Dr Ludlow, from his uneasy perch on the arm of an easy chair, nodded approval.

"Better if you can. Enough dirty linen will be washed in public without adding to it. And there is a practical consideration too. Half Shropshire and Cheshire will be coming to the funeral. You can't upset the domestic arrangements here until all that is dealt with."

Rosalie passed a hand over her eyes.

"Heavens! I hadn't given that a thought. You are right, of course, although we would manage somehow." She glanced at her son. "All the same, I think that Mrs Lightfoot should be given notice, Roderick, as soon as possible."

"I don't think she will want to stay, anyway," he replied, thoughtfully, "She'll be off, without us having to give her the boot. Fresh woods, you know. And I'm too young for her." He glanced at his watch. "I'd better be moving. Old thingummy's train will be in Oldchurch in half an hour. You feel like a run out, Marion? Do you good."

The pale face lit up momentarily.

"Oh, yes, I would, Rod."

"Come on then."

They went out together.

Dr Ludlow looked after them speculatively.

"Anything doing there, do you think?"

Rosalie shook her head.

"For all you have known Roderick all his life, Geoffrey, you don't know much about him."

"Marion is an attractive girl. And how old is Roderick? Twenty-three, isn't he? Time enough for him to be thinking of marriage."

"He'll marry when he is good and ready. And, you mark my words, she will be some girl with a face like a horse, a pedigree as long as your arm, and money."

Ludlow stared at her.

"You do surprise me."

"I understand Roderick," Rosalie smiled, "He may look like me, but that is as far as it goes. His roots are here. In Astonley.

"And now it will be his."

"Yes. I imagine we shall move out of the Dower House after the funeral." She glanced round at the room, with its ancient and valuable contents. "I never expected Roderick to succeed. Not with James healthy and married. It takes a bit of getting used to."

She was thinking: it will never be my home; I've waited twenty years to escape, back to where I belong; Roderick doesn't need me; I am free to go.

"I suppose nothing has ever been heard of George?"

Ludlow's question jolted her out of a pleasant little reverie. She had not thought of her late husband's other brother for many a year.

"He died ages ago. Drank himself to death somewhere, I believe. I never knew him. He had kicked over the traces long before I married Arthur. No one ever mentioned him in Robert's hearing."

"Not surprising," commented Ludlow darkly. He remembered George Winter only too well. A bad egg if ever there was one. And his two other brothers, Denis and Arthur, such decent fellows. Dead now, all three of them. And their old father, too.

Geoffrey Ludlow felt chilled and old himself.

Rosalie stood up.

"This won't do, idling about. You gathered it was Mr Walters whom Roderick has gone to meet off the train? He insisted on coming himself, and he will stay until after the funeral, though he is really too old to be traipsing round the countryside. He's well over eighty, you know, and still goes into his office in Lincoln's Inn three days a week. There must be something about the law which acts as a preservative."

Ludlow followed her into the hall.

And there was Mrs Lightfoot.

Rosalie stopped.

"May I ask if you and Mr Roderick will be staying here tonight, Mrs Winter? Or will you be moving back home?"

"We will be staying, of course. Someone has to entertain Mr Walters," Rosalie told her, coldly, "I hope his room is ready."

"It is. The South Room, as you suggested, Mrs Winter."

Without another word, the woman turned her back and left them.

Rosalie swung round, her eyes blazing.

"The sooner she goes, the better." Then her anger evaporated and a rueful smile appeared. "It's ridiculous, Geoffrey. I've never wanted to be mistress of Astonley. You know that. I don't even like living in the country. But the way that woman treats me as a stranger—an interloper —in my father-in-law's house—my son's house now—never fails to rile me. If Roderick keeps her on, I shall have something to say about it."

Ludlow frowned.

"What did he mean, just now, when he said that she wouldn't want to stay on? That—what were the words?—that he was too young for her?"

Rosalie laughed outright.

"Geoffrey, are you blind? I should have thought anyone could have seen that our Mrs Lightfoot is what used to be described as 'superior'. I don't imagine that she considered going into domestic service until she was left a widow. Her husband was a Civil Servant of some sort. She fancies herself as the comfort of some rich old man, preferably ending in marriage, or at least, in a sizeable inheritance. That's why she can't bear Marion. She hadn't a chance of worming her way into Robert's affections while Marion was there. And—" she broke off, staring out through the open door ahead of them, into the formal garden, which lay on the south of the house.

Marion Loring was walking up the path.

Rosalie ran out.

"Marion! I thought you had gone with Roderick?"

Marion shook her head.

"I was going to, but there was a message."

She got no further. A brisk step sounded on the flags, and Inspector Morton came round the side of the house.

"Ah! there you are, Miss Loring. Sorry to stop you when you were just going out," he said with false geniality, "Just a few more questions."

CHAPTER 4

MARION said bitterly, "I suppose you have been listening to Mrs Lightfoot."

"I could scarcely do anything else," Morton retorted grimly, "You forget that I was in the house this morning when she started yelling at you. The noise brought everyone in earshot into the hall to see what was going on."

There was no answer to that one. Without further comment, Marion followed the Inspector into the house.

"Which room can we use?" he asked, glancing back at her.

It was Rosalie who answered him, following anxiously, with Dr Ludlow.

"The study. The door opposite the drawingroom. Marion, dear, would you like me to stay with you?"

"I'm sorry," Morton said flatly, "I wish to interview Miss Loring alone."

"Oh," for a moment Rosalie seemed taken aback, "I'll be in the drawingroom, Marion."

The girl flashed her a grateful look before following Inspector Morton into the study. It was still something of a surprise, this support from Aunt Rosalie. She had always been kind, but in a rather off-hand way, confidences neither invited nor offered. But a change had set in, right after James's death. Marion had no idea what had brought it about, but she was glad of it. It was a comfort to know that she was not entirely alone.

Morton took the big chair behind the desk. Uncle

Robert's chair, Marion thought resentfully, which he had no right to appropriate. But she said nothing, slipping into the place he indicated, directly in front of him.

"I have to investigate Mrs Lightfoot's charges, you know," he began, not unkindly, "They may well be rooted in spite. What has she against you?"

"I don't know. We have never got on together. But I had no idea that she felt like that about me."

"The substance of her charge, Miss Loring—and I would like to point out that she makes it in all seriousness: there is no element of hysteria in this—is that you despatched that telegram knowing that its contents would be sufficient to bring on another stroke and so kill Mr Robert Winter."

"But it's fantastic!" Marion exclaimed, "How could I have done?"

Morton gazed at her.

"Oh, you could have done it all right. That telegram was handed in in London last night, at five-thirty p.m. It was sent by the overnight rate, so it was bound to be delivered the following morning. You were in London that day, weren't you?"

Marion nodded.

"Yes. You know I was. I was with Aunt Rosalie and Roderick. We had to go to that beastly inquest."

"So you did. The resumed inquest on Mr James Winter and his wife, Alice. And were the three of you together the whole day?"

Marion hesitated.

"Were you?" he pressed her.

"No," she admitted reluctantly, "We split up after the inquest. We met at the train, in the evening."

"And what did you do with yourself? How long had you?"

Marion sighed.

"About three hours, I suppose. I looked round the shops."

"On your own?"

"Yes."

"So you see what I mean? You could have sent that telegram, couldn't you?"

Marion stared at him angrily, but after a moment her eyes dropped.

"What if I could? I didn't. I loved Uncle Robert. He had taken me in, given me a home, educated me. Everything."

"Ah, yes, you aren't a blood relative?"

"No. He was my godfather. My father was the vicar, down in the village. He and Uncle Robert were up at Oxford together. They were very close friends. So when my father married, late in life, and then I arrived, naturally he was my godfather. My mother died when I was three, and my father when I was ten. Uncle Robert took me in."

Morton made a few jottings in his notebook, while Marion watched him, fascinated.

"And lately you have been acting as Mr Winter's secretary. For how long?"

"For the past three years."

"Since you left school? Or have you had another job?"

Marion shook her head.

"I took a commercial course after I left school, then came straight back here. Uncle Robert didn't think it was necessary, but I'm glad that I did take it now. At least I can earn my living."

"Do you honestly think you have to?"

"I don't understand."

"Surely, your godfather will have made provision for you in his will?"

"I have no idea. He never discussed it with me."

"Really?"

Marion felt her face flame at the sheer disbelief in his tone.

"It's the truth."

Morton stared hard at her for a moment.

"I imagine there is only your word for it," he said at last. "There is no use our arguing about it. Let's get back to this telegram. When it arrived it was brought to you. Why didn't you open it?"

"Uncle Robert was expecting a telegram. He told me not to open it when it arrived but to bring it straight to him."

"Was that usual?"

"No. I was surprised."

"And what was this other telegram about?"

"I've no idea. Uncle Robert wouldn't tell me. But he seemed quite cheerful about it. I was glad about that. There wasn't much to be cheerful about, just then."

"Quite so. This was just after the murder of his son and daughter-in-law in London?"

"Yes."

"And you know absolutely nothing about this other telegram? Has it turned up?"

Marion shook her head.

"No. I did wonder if it might be connected with a letter which Uncle Robert received from his solicitor, Mr Walters, a few days earlier."

"And what was in that letter?"

"I don't know. Uncle Robert always opened letters from Mr Walters himself. The envelopes were easy to pick out. There is the stamp of the firm on the back."

"And where did he keep those letters?"

"In his desk. You have the keys," she added, almost accusingly, "You locked up the desk this morning."

Morton permitted himself a little satisfied smile. It had been a piece of luck for him to be at the house when the old man died.

"So I have. Though I have no doubt that Mr Walters himself will tell me. I understand he is on his way here."

"Yes. Roderick has driven into Oldchurch to meet his train."

Morton made another jotting in his little book.

"Right, Miss Loring," he said briskly, "let us proceed. We have established that you had the opportunity to send that telegram, and also that you could be sure that you would be the one to handle it when it arrived here, and that Mr Winter himself would open it and so get the full shock of the contents."

Marion eyed him angrily, but said nothing. There was no point.

"Now, Miss Loring, if the text of the message is to be believed, the person who sent that telegram was also the person who sent the anonymous letter, six weeks ago, and who also broke into the Winters' home in London, and planted a good dose of arsenic in their food." Morton paused, but the girl offered no comment. "Let's have a look at the dates involved. The anonymous letter was posted in London on May 3rd. Can you remember where you were on that date?"

Marion found that her hands had balled into tight fists.

"No," she replied.

"Then let me refresh your memory. On May the first, you went to London, to stay with a school friend. You returned here on May the fourth. Had you forgotten that?"

Marion flushed.

"I—I mixed the dates," she stammered.

"Yet you came back to Astonley to find a full-scale campaign going on to find the sender of that letter. I should have thought those dates would have been fixed in your mind."

If only you knew! she thought. How could I ever forget? Aloud, she said nothing.

"Can your friend account for every moment of your stay with her? Were you together all the time?"

Marion shook her head. As if he didn't know!

"So you could have sent the telegram," Morton continued smoothly, "and you could have sent the letter. There remains the matter of the break-in at James Winter's home. That took place on the second of June. And once again, you were in London. And further, you must have known that the London house would be empty. James Winter and his wife had come into Shropshire for the weekend to visit his grandfather at Astonley. And this time you didn't stay with your friend, but in a hotel. Alone. How about that, Miss Loring?"

Marion's head was whirling. It was all a series of the most ghastly coincidences. And she dared not explain. No use handing him a motive on a plate.

"But it doesn't mean anything," she blurted, "You've got it all wrong."

Morton raised an incredulous eyebrow.

"One of the things we look for, Miss Loring, when we are investigating a case of murder, is an unaccountable change in a pattern of behaviour. Now, take your case. You've lived in this village all your life, and in this house for the past twelve years. The only times that you have been away have been holidays and your schooldays. When you finished your education, you came back here. All, apparently, as before. Then, suddenly, at the beginning of May—only a few days after the receipt of that letter—you apply for a job in London."

Marion thought dejectedly: they were bound to get on to that; I had made no secret of it.

"Why, Miss Loring?"

"I felt I needed a change."

"And yet your godfather was partially paralysed from his first stroke, last year, and, I gather, was a good deal dependent on you. Yet you were preparing to leave Astonley."

"Yes." Marion felt the blood come up into her face, "That was why I was in London at the beginning of June. I went for an interview."

How she had blessed that interview, at the time, for the so reasonable excuse which it had given her to be away from Astonley!

"Did you get the job?" Morton was asking.

"No."

There was a silence, while Inspector Morton looked over his witness speculatively. Marion tried to meet his eyes, but could not. She began to tremble.

"You know, there is one thing which I find puzzling, Miss Loring," he said, just when the silence had become unbearable, and she almost gasped in relief. "There has to be a motive for murder. We have touched on the matter of your godfather's will, and, although you won't admit it, I am quite sure that he won't have left you with nothing. But that doesn't provide any sort of motive for killing off James Winter and his wife. I would have expected you to challenge me on that one. But you haven't."

Marion's mouth was dry and she could not speak. She shook her head.

"I've my own ideas on that," he went on, "It wasn't all that difficult to put two and two together. Before long, I expect to have the whole story."

Someone was ringing the front door bell, a long and exuberant peal. Morton started up, crossed to the window, opened it and leaned out. From there he could look along the west front of the house.

A Post Office motor cycle was propped against the porch. Morton left the window.

"I'll see what that is. It looks like a telegram. It's a bit early for condolences to be coming in. Who knows, Miss

Loring? It might be that mysterious other telegram that Mr Winter was expecting. Perhaps you didn't invent it, after all."

Marion was at his heels as he crossed the hall, to take the familiar buff envelope from a startled maid.

"I'll take charge of this, Miss," he said grimly, "Where's Mrs Winter?"

"I'm here," said Rosalie, before the girl could reply. "I heard the commotion. What is it?"

"A telegram, madam. Addressed to Winter. Might be for any one of you. I'm going to open it."

Rosalie inclined her head.

"As you wish, Inspector," she replied coldly.

Morton tore open the envelope.

He glanced at the message, then passed it to Rosalie, with a shrug.

Rosalie read it, then looked up.

"But I don't understand this," she said blankly, "Look, Marion."

The girl took the flimsy paper.

It read:

"ARRIVING ENGLAND MONDAY WILL COME STRAIGHT TO ASTONLEY"

"It's signed Thomas," she said, "Who's he?"

CHAPTER 5

MARION slipped quietly away from the little group in the hall. If Inspector Morton saw her go, he said nothing. He was more intent on questioning Rosalie over the telegram. Marion went out into the walled garden, half-fearful lest she might be called back.

Once outside the house, she breathed more freely. She knew the Inspector had not finished with her, but any respite was welcome. For the second time in her life, Astonley, with all its splendour, had turned into a trap.

The second time. . . .

Unavoidably, her mind dodged back treacherously to that first occasion, when all that she loved had suddenly turned to dust and ashes.

She began to run.

She found herself at the far side of the garden, where the iron gates stood open to the park. She ran on, through them, out into the meadows. She came to a cart track and turned along it, walking now that the immediate urge to escape was satisfied. The track followed an irregular line of trees, between fields green with the harvest to come. The afternoon sun shone serenely through the leaves, making patterns on the dry rutted ground.

Marion fell to thinking about the latest telegram, and its unknown sender. It must be the one which Uncle Robert had been expecting. More than expecting. Looking forward to. And important. So important that he must open it himself, so that no one should know its contents until he chose to reveal them.

And she had welcomed the idea. Anything which might cheer him up, and take his mind off the horrors of murder. How glad she had been to see the telegraph boy that morning! She had even rejoiced that it had come when she was there to take it in. And Uncle Robert had been pathetically happy to receive the loathsome little envelope. Which made the shock so much worse.

And who was Thomas? It might even be a woman, she thought, suddenly; it could just as easily be a surname as a Christian name. Uncle Robert had never mentioned a Thomas.

The cart track ended at a farm gate. Beyond it lay a huddle of barns and a neat, square early Victorian house. Marion, recognising that her feet had brought her to a sure source of comfort, pushed open the gate, and made her way into the house. The back door leading into the big kitchen was open, as usual, and inside, a plump middle-aged woman in a bright flowered overall was at the sink preparing vegetables.

"Is Mr David in?" asked Marion.

The woman smiled.

"In the office, Miss Marion."

Originally, it had been the parlour. Now it was converted as the land agent's office, a comfortable crowded mess of desk and filing cabinets, all overflowing with farming periodicals. By the fireplace were a couple of armchairs. Beside one was a small table bearing a large ashtray, a pipe and a book. In spite of the well-furnished sittingroom across the hall, David Kenyon-Winter preferred to spend his evenings reading and smoking in his office.

He was at the desk now, poring over a bundle of forms. He glanced up quickly as Marion came in, his expression of annoyance no more than a passing flash.

"Oh, it's you, Marion. Come in."

"I don't want to interrupt you," she replied hesitantly.

He pushed aside the papers.

"You aren't. These can wait." He stepped forward. "My dear girl, what is the matter?"

He reached for her hands, and pulled her gently towards one of the chairs.

"You're icy cold. Here, sit down."

Marion subsided into the chair, while David put his head round the door and shouted to his housekeeper to make a pot of tea.

"Now," he said firmly, turning back into the room, "tell me."

No wonder that her feet had led her here, she thought, looking up into the kind, familiar face! She could not remember a time when David had not been there, to console or advise. He was part of Astonley just as Uncle Robert or the house itself. But Uncle Robert was dead and the house had become unbearable. Only David was unchanged.

It was a relief to pour out to him the story of the ghastly interview with Inspector Morton.

"He as good as told me that he could work out a motive for me," she ended desolately.

David frowned.

"No one knowing you could possibly believe it."

"But Inspector Morton doesn't know me," she pointed out, "and there's another thing." She looked up at him, standing squarely before her, as reliable as a rock. "I was hating James—before he died."

David turned away from her abruptly.

"Marion!"

"It's true," she replied steadily, "I know that it seems impossible, after all these years. But love can turn to hate. I know. It's happened to me."

He walked over to the window, stood staring out.

"I had hoped that you were over all that."

"I tried, David. It wasn't that I didn't try."

He swung round.

"James wasn't your sort, Marion. He'd have made you a rotten husband."

"I know that now. But I loved him, David."

"It was his mother's fault. She put the idea into everyone's head. Yours included."

His face was in shadow, against the strong light from the window, but it seemed to Marion that David was angry.

"Oh, no," she protested, "I didn't imagine myself into falling in love."

"You were an impressionable girl, fifteen, when she started on the subject. James's mother was only half a fool, you know. She wasn't blind to his faults. She knew he was wild. Heavens! we all did."

"I didn't," said Marion, in a small voice.

"No, we kept it from you. A mistake, in my opinion. He was up at Oxford at that time, and he was all but sent down. That's when his mother decided you would be a settling influence. And Robert agreed with her. He was thinking of Astonley and seeing the pair of you well established. He should have known better, but he couldn't see James as he was. Only as he wanted him to be. James was bound to gravitate to the Alices of this world."

"David! She's dead!" Marion protested.

"That doesn't change her character," he pointed out, "I didn't like her particularly, but she was full of life and enjoying herself, and I'm sorry for her that it was ended so soon. But it doesn't turn her into a saint. Could you honestly imagine her as mistress of Astonley? Do her justice. Alice herself was frankly appalled at the prospect. She hated living in the country."

In spite of herself, Marion had to smile. Oddly, she had liked Alice. There was a forthrightness about her which appealed. In the end there was even a sort of fellow-feeling, born of the moment when Marion had seen James in his true colours.

"Yes," she admitted, "I was forgetting what she was really like. Poor Alice!"

"Poor James," he added softly, watching her.

"That too," Marion replied steadily, "I can't feel anything for him now. He might just as well have been a stranger. Not that that is any help to me. Not with Mrs Lightfoot spreading the story that I killed James and Alice to get my own back on them. There are plenty of people who can testify how I reacted to James's marriage."

David nodded.

"It was a shock for all of us, him turning up like that, with a wife in tow. Inexcusable, to my mind. He knew what the score was here."

"They were so far away. He'd met her in Capetown."

"He could have written. Or cabled. Anything to prepare you for it. They had been married a month before they arrived at Astonley. I'm afraid, Marion, that it was all deliberate."

Even now, it hurt to remember that morning, when the joyful anticipation of James's return was turned in an instant into heart-break.

"Don't let's talk about it."

"We have to," he insisted, "Inspector Morton will be raking all this over. But there is one point that you—and he—seem to be missing."

"What's that?"

"If you wanted to revenge yourself on James, why wait the best part of two years to do it?"

Marion shook her head.

"You don't know the half of it. Dr Ludlow hustled Mrs Lightfoot out of Uncle Robert's room this morning before she had said the whole of her piece. The rest of it is that I have been trying to get James back—and I've failed."

"But that is ridiculous."

Marion looked away quickly. She had caught a tiny hint of uncertainty in his tone. Suddenly, there were barriers between them.

"I'll have to go," she said hurriedly, "Mr Walters will have arrived."

There was a rattle of a tray and crockery outside the door.

"Here's the tea," David announced, unnecessarily, "Stay and have a cup now it is made."

She would never have believed it possible, that she and David could sit drinking tea like a couple of strangers sharing a table by chance. She caught herself staring at him, as if seeing him for the first time. He wasn't actually good-looking, she decided, but solid and dependable. She wondered why he had never married. He must be thirty-eight, at least.

"If you want to get away from Astonley for a while," he said, breaking the awkward silence, "my sister would be happy to have you to stay with her in Bristol."

Ten minutes ago, she would have fallen on his neck in gratitude.

"That's very kind of her," she replied, "And you, for thinking of it. But I think I had better stay here, all the same."

Until she could escape altogether, she told herself. At the moment, she felt that her last prop had been taken from her, her last link with Astonley broken. And all for one little implied question which had succeeded in shattering their long relationship. Now she was on her own.

She fled back towards Astonley. There was nowhere else to go—for the time being. But they were finished now, the glorious years. The sooner she could lose herself in the uncaring world of the City, the better.

She arrived in the hall as Mr Walters, his old bones creaking with the fatigue of his journey, was being helped out of the car, drawn up before the open front door. He was complaining about the lateness of the train, and taking in, with one shrewd glance, the faces of those around him.

"Rosalie, my dear," he murmured, "You must tell Roderick to drive more slowly. Most dangerous. And is that Marion, in the hall? And who is this gentleman?"

Rosalie sighed.

"Inspector Morton."

"Quite so," nodded Mr Walters, and allowed Roderick to lead him into the house. "Ah, there you are, Marion. How are you, child?"

Marion could scarcely repress the shudder which ran through her body as the old claw-like hand closed on her arm. The lawyer had always frightened her, when she was a child. An old vulture with sharp eyes which had looked on every sin in the world.

To cover it, she blurted the first thought in her head.

"Mr Walters, we've had a peculiar telegram. From some-one called Thomas."

There was an exclamation of annoyance from Rosalie. Mr Walters did not heed it. He peered at Marion.

"So it's come, has it?"

In spite of her conviction that this was neither the time nor the place to open the matter, Rosalie found herself waiting for the lawyer to explain.

"What's all this?" demanded Roderick.

No one answered him.

"So you do know about it?" said Marion.

"Oh, yes," agreed Mr Walters cheerfully. A gleam of malicious amusement came into his eyes. "Thomas," he said, looking at each in turn, until he reached Roderick, where his gaze rested, "Thomas is the heir to Astonley."

CHAPTER 6

"I WAS glad I was there," said Inspector Morton, "Mind you, I had the impression that that old devil intended to spring his bombshell on them in front of witnesses. As it was, they played right into his hands."

He took a deep pull at a pint of beer which he felt had been truly earned, and gazed round at the cosy old bar of the "White Swan", the pub next to the church in Winsmere. It was barely half-past six and the place was empty. Which suited Inspector Morton.

He cocked an inquiring eyebrow at his companion.

Charles Warren returned his gaze blandly. He was well aware that there was an ulterior motive in the Inspector's seemingly casual invitation down to the local for a pint. Morton was no plodding flatfoot, but a subtle, successful hunter of men. It was a pity that all senior policemen whom he met in the course of his work did not take a lesson or two from Morton.

"Shocks all round?"

Morton nodded.

"Without a doubt. That young Roderick. Covered up very well, but it shook him. And his mother."

"How is it that no one had ever heard of this—what was his name?—Thomas?"

"The solicitor explained it all, and with a good deal of relish. I don't know what he has against that family, but he enjoyed every moment of it. Might have been malice for the sheer hell of it. Anyway, what it boils down to is this.

The old man who died this morning, Robert Winter, had three sons. The eldest Denis died young, leaving a widow and a baby son, James. Old Robert promptly took them in, and they lived with him at Astonley, until the mother died five years ago, and James— Well, you know about James Winter. The youngest son, Arthur, was a steady type. Hard worker. He worked too hard, in fact. He was a barrister, and ambitious. But it didn't do him any good, poor fellow. His health broke, so he came home, bringing his wife and family with him. They took the Dower House."

"Just a minute," Charles broke in, "That is Mrs Rosalie Winter and Roderick?"

"Yes. The husband didn't last long, and they stayed on in the Dower House. There's a daughter, too, but she married an American last year and lives in Washington. Which brings us to the remaining son, the middle one, George. A real stinker, from all accounts. He had a grand bust-up with his father, thirty years ago and more. And off he went."

"Where to?"

"Heaven knows. He certainly didn't stay in England. Nothing more was heard of him, until about fifteen years ago, a letter turned up at Astonley, from a woman who claimed to be George's wife, or, rather, his widow, announcing that George had died in Australia."

"And what did old Robert do about that?" asked Charles.

"Nothing. He handed the letter over to Mr Walters, instructing him to write back to the woman informing her that she was mistaken; George Winter was nothing to do with the Winters of Astonley. It was a pretty illiterate letter, and I gather he thought it could be an attempt at a shake-down. And even if it was genuine, he wasn't interested."

"And I suppose that this Thomas is George's son?"

"He is," Morton confirmed, "Though, as far as I can

make out, he knew nothing of Astonley until a few months ago. Until, in fact, he was approached by Robert Winter's solicitors."

Charles's eyebrows shot up.

"So the old man changed his mind?"

"He did. You know he had his first stroke last year. Well, it gave him an attack of conscience. He felt he should have done something for George's widow, no matter who she was. So he told Mr Walters to find her."

"In Australia?"

"Yes. He contacted a legal firm over there, and left the matter to them. She had left her old address, but they found her. She had married again, and couldn't have cared less about Robert Winter and his tender conscience. But she did suggest that he might do something for her son Thomas, his grandson."

"So the missing heir turned out to be from Down Under. All very romantic," Charles commented.

Morton laughed.

"Sounds like a story book, doesn't it? Oddly enough, Thomas didn't see eye to eye with his mother, left home and has been living in England for years. Mr Walters found him in Bristol. But he has been on a visit to America for the past three months. When James Winter died, old Robert decided that he wanted Thomas to come to Astonley at once, and sent for him."

Inspector Morton grinned. "He's arriving on Monday. I wonder what sort of reception he will get?"

"So, in fact," said Charles thoughtfully, "If these murders were done to get hold of the estate, then somebody has received a very nasty shock indeed. What sort of a place is Astonley? I haven't been up there yet."

"It's a showplace. Fifteenth century manor house. Great hall, minstrels' gallery, oak panelling. The lot. And plenty of cash to keep it up, too. I'll admit that my first thought was to wonder who would be the lucky one. Until this afternoon, I thought it would be Roderick Winter. So did everyone else. Including him. The place is entailed, with the succession in the male line. The Winters have had it for a couple of hundred years and they don't intend to let go of it."

"How does Roderick rate as a suspect? The motive is there, even though it turns out that he doesn't get the place after all. He thought he would."

Morton smiled ruefully.

"I've only had this case a day and a half. Since that telegram arrived yesterday morning. I seem to be spending most of my waking hours at Astonley. And I am handicapped by the fact that the first two murders—James and his wife—were committed in London. Right out of my area. From what I can gather, there could have been any amount of folks willing to see the back of James Winter. He was that sort. But this way, with the anonymous letter and then the telegram, deliberately playing on his grandfather's health—that points to the roots of the thing being among the Winters themselves, here at Astonley, or with some very close connection."

"And you are not happy about it?"

Morton shook his head.

"There are a lot of things I'm not happy about at the moment," he said darkly, "Take the matter as a whole, and as far as I can see the motive behind it has to be one of two things : either spite; or money. And what have we got? The girl, Marion Loring, apparently brought up to believe that she would marry James Winter, who I gather played a very dirty trick on her and the rest of them by springing a wife on them unannounced. That's the spite angle. By all accounts she was devoted to the old man, but she may well have felt that he had deceived her. They say love can turn to hate. Then, the money. Roderick Winter sticks out a mile. He gets the jackpot. But I've had a glance at the old man's will, disposing of the property which isn't entailed. No one has been forgotten. They all get something, the family and the servants and the workers on the estate. So much for each year's service. You know the sort of thing. And it mounts up to a tidy sum for those who've been at Astonley a while."

"So it amounts to this : who had the opportunity to send the letter, poison the fruit in James's house, and send the telegram? London in every case. We are a fair distance from Town here. It shouldn't be very difficult to eliminate a number of people."

"Only too easy," agreed Morton, "I'll go even further. There was only one person who lives at Astonley who was in London about the right times for all three. And that was Miss Loring. But several of the others have visited London on one or more of the relevant dates."

"So you can't rule out collusion between any two of them?"

"That's right, Mr Warren. And how the hell do you prove that any particular person posted a particular letter or sent a particular telegram from a busy central post office?"

"You can't."

"Quite. Our best bet is the break-in at James Winter's place. But they have been working on that for a fortnight and haven't come up with a lead yet. Not that it is really my pigeon," Morton added carefully.

Charles suppressed a smile. He had been flattered at receiving the Inspector's confidence, but equally sure that there was something behind it. Now it was appearing.

"No?" he prompted, gently.

"With the case split between here and London, the proper thing is for Scotland Yard to take over," Morton sounded as if he were reciting from a police manual.

So that was it. Morton did not welcome the idea of being

superseded by the London man, and would give his eye teeth to crack the case before he could arrive on the scene. And was willing to go to any lengths—even to picking the brains of the Ministry of Security official who happened to be on hand.

"I'm sorry," he said, genuinely regretful, "but I can't help you. I know these people no better than you do. This is my first visit here. But I'll sound out my wife. She knows them."

Morton smiled briefly.

"Thanks."

"Who is taking over?"

"Superintendent Beech," Morton replied, his face wooden.

Charles was doubly sorry that he could offer no substantial help to Morton. It would have given him great pleasure to have assisted him to wipe the eye of Superintendent Reginald Beech.

"Do you know him?" he asked.

"Yes," came the reply, still wooden, "I worked with him a year or two back on a case near Chester."

"I came across him in a little matter I was dealing with a few months ago," Charles grinned at him.

Morton relaxed.

"Proper bastard, isn't he?"

CHAPTER 7

"It is completely out of the question," said Rosalie Winter firmly, and to nobody in particular, "None of us is free to go and meet Thomas. We don't even know which port he will be landing at, though I suppose it will be Southampton."

"We could find out," Roderick suggested, more to goad his mother than to lay out a welcome for the missing heir.

Rosalie glared at him.

"I think it is most inconsiderate. He could have given us more warning. That cable was sent from somewhere in mid-Atlantic. I fail to see why he could not have sent it off before he left New York. Monday! I imagine that means that he will be here by Monday evening or Tuesday morning at the latest. And today is Saturday. But I suppose," she went on bitterly, "that it was too much to expect the smallest consideration from any child of George."

There was no answer to that one. Every person in the room understood her unspoken thought: that it was very inconsiderate of George to have produced a son at all.

They had gathered in the drawingroom, following the normal course of an evening at Astonley, for sherry before dinner, but it was all changed, and the routine seemed unnatural, conversation difficult. Even David, unusually, had broken his habit and accepted an invitation to dine. Marion reckoned that she could count on one hand the number of times each year that David spent the evening at Astonley. He preferred his quiet bachelor establishment.

The four of them sat stiffly, each unwilling to broach the subject uppermost in their minds.

Thomas Winter.

Then Rosalie, in the middle of a one-sided discussion with David of the coming church fete, broke off, gazed round at all of them and made her observations concerning the arrival of the heir.

It was a relief to them all.

"I wonder what he will be like," Marion ventured.

"Ghastly," Roderick assured her, with a broad grin, "An Aussie, brought up the Lord knows where."

In spite of the grin, there was an edge to his voice, and Rosalie frowned at her son.

"Don't be ridiculous. We can't judge him before we see him. No matter what he is like, Roderick, you will have to watch your step now. If you want to stay on in the Dower House, that is."

Roderick's grin broadened.

"Hear that, David?"

David calmly shook out his pipe.

"I don't see that it affects me. I don't want to leave Astonley, but if I don't see eye to eye with Thomas, I will. After all, I'm only an employee."

"You're a cousin, too."

"Agreed. We all share the same great-grandfather. To my mind that is remote enough. And I don't live here in my capacity as a relative. I work here. If Thomas doesn't like me, that's that. I can work where I please."

"Which is more than you can say, Roderick," Rosalie joined in sharply, "For some reason best known to himself, your grandfather was quite willing for you to idle about here. Just as he encouraged James to laze about. Good for neither of you."

"I'm not idle," Roderick protested, "I give David a hand with the work of the estate. Don't I, David?"

"At times."

This was an old argument, which had often raged, but always behind Robert Winter's back. Marion had heard it all so many times, knew every turn which it would take, but had never taken part in it herself. But Robert Winter was dead now. In his lifetime, he had been too proud to explain himself to his daughter-in-law. In death, Marion must speak for him.

"David is being charitable," Rosalie was saying, "I can't think that either you or James was ever much help to him."

"It's not fair to blame Roderick, Aunt Rosalie," Marion struck in, and three pairs of astonished eyes gazed at her. "Or James, either. Uncle Robert didn't want them to make careers for themselves. That would have taken them away from Astonley. That was one of the things he held against poor Alice. Because she insisted on James living in London."

"He could have stopped his allowance. Then he would have had to stay on here," said Rosalie bitterly, before she could stop herself. She was ashamed to find that she could still feel jealousy over that, even when the girl was in her grave.

"Not like you, Mother dear," said Roderick softly, his eyes sharp with malice. "Grandpa made very sure that you stayed here, didn't he? It amused him to hear you complaining about the country."

Rosalie had regained control.

"That is quite enough of that," she said coldly. She turned to Marion, "Would you mind going up to Nora's room, to fetch her down? It is ridiculous for her to go on taking her meals alone, when there is no patient for her to look after. And she will only be here for another few days. And we can't very well put her into the servants' hall. But she may feel a bit strange about it. So, if you don't mind, Marion?"

"No, of course not. I'll be glad to."

Marion slipped out of the room, happy to be out of the bickering. Knowing Roderick, he would be unlikely to let the matter rest. She ran lightly up the stairs, thinking how easy it was to find oneself in an impossible situation, especially as a result of marriage.

Poor Aunt Rosalie, a town girl by birth and by choice, stuck in a remote corner of Shropshire for twenty-odd years. And all through falling in love with a rising young barrister, whom she could reasonably have expected to live in Town for the rest of his days. It was unkind of Roderick to make out that his mother had stayed on at Astonley only because the old man held the purse strings, although that was undoubtedly part of it. But Rosalie had put Roderick's interests before her own. It occurred to Marion that Rosalie had not made many friends in the district. The only ones she could recall, off-hand, were Dr Ludlow and his wife. Since Mrs Ludlow's death, Rosalie must have been lonely.

She tapped on Nora Deeping's door, and was bidden to come in.

"Oh, it's you, Marion."

"We wondered where you were. We are all in the drawingroom. Aunt Rosalie sent me to bring you down."

Nora smiled.

"That's very kind of her. I shan't keep you a minute. I was just going through a couple of drawers. It's amazing what I've accumulated. Sit down for a moment."

One of the drawers from the tallboy was on the bed, its contents strewn over the coverlet.

"I'll just put this lot back," Nora was saying, "I should hate to find it all waiting for me later."

Marion found herself a chair near the window. Beside it was a small heap of articles, papers, clothes, shoes and plastic bags, all obviously intended for throwing out. Idly, she picked out a newspaper, and began glancing through it, while Nora worked swiftly to put her things back in place.

"I thought I had better get on with this," Nora said, sliding the drawer back into the tallboy base, "It always takes so much longer than one expects. And I have been here over a year."

Marion looked up. The newspaper was old and uninteresting.

"Where will you go?"

"Home, for a bit. I'll treat myself to a fortnight's holiday and live it up. Dear old London! Though, I must say, in lots of ways, I shall miss Astonley.

For the first time, Marion warmed towards Nora. The nurse had changed. She had put off her uniform and, with it, the slightly officious manner which had repelled Marion. And there was a cheerfulness about her which was a welcome relief.

"I suppose you get used to people dying, in your profession."

Nora cast her a shrewd glance.

"You have to," she replied, in a matter-of-fact tone, "I'm sorry when I lose a patient, naturally, but in a case like this one, you know, it was only to be expected. He couldn't have lasted long anyway. I have been expecting him to have another stroke at any time over these past few months." She glanced round the room. "Whatever my next job is, it will be a come-down after this."

There was real regret in her tone.

"Oh, well, come on," she went on briskly, "I'm keeping everyone waiting."

They were at the head of the stairs when Marion felt a sudden jerk at her shoulder.

"Bother!" she exclaimed, "My slip strap has broken. I'll have to put a pin in it. You go on down. I shan't be a tick."

She ran into her own bedroom.

She discovered that she was still holding the old newspaper which she had picked up in Nora's room, flung it in the direction of the bed, missed and saw it slide smoothly across the polished boards and under the daintily draped four-poster. With an exclamation of annoyance, she left it, to hunt on her dressing table for a pin to fix her shoulder strap.

Downstairs once more, Marion realised that, in the short time that she had been gone, more trouble had brewed up. And from the impish expression on his face, all of it Roderick's fault. Rosalie looked furious. David frowned. Nora watched all three of them warily.

"Ah, Marion, here you are!" Rosalie's eyes were fixed on her son as she spoke, "Now Roderick, this subject has to be dropped."

"No, Mother, I don't agree."

"It's not fair to Marion."

"You'll have to tell her what we've been discussing now, Mother," he crowed triumphantly, "You can't leave it at that. Can she, Marion. You want to know what we have been saying about you, don't you?"

Marion gazed round at them. No one, except Roderick, would meet her eyes.

"I think I can guess," she said faintly.

In an instant, David was out of his chair and at her side.

"Come and sit down," he said gently, and guided her to the settee where he sat down beside her. "We aren't as bad as you might think, Marion. We weren't only discussing you. We were working out which of us were in a position to send that letter, break into James's house and send that telegram."

"Roderick was, you mean," Rosalie cut in bleakly.

"All right, Roderick raised the subject. I didn't agree that we should discuss this, but since he has started it, then perhaps it would be just as well to bring it out into the open."

Marion could only stare at him. She wondered if they had already reached the same conclusion as the police; that she was the only one. But she couldn't put it into words. These people, already half-strangers, were all the family she had. She dreaded the moment when they, too, would accuse her.

"The police aren't fools, Mother," Roderick was thoroughly enjoying himself, "Certainly that Inspector Morton can see beyond the end of his nose. There are three dates which matter. The third of May, the second of June and last Thursday. Marion had the bad luck to be in London on all three days. But she's too obvious. Heavens! at that rate, she might as well have signed that telegram."

Help. And from such an unexpected quarter. Marion gazed at Roderick, ashamed for all the times when she had found him irritating almost beyond endurance.

He grinned back at her.

"Morton may spend a lot of time grilling Marion. He has to, after darling Lightfoot's outburst, but don't any of you believe that it will distract his attention from you. We've all got motives, and better ones than Marion trying to revenge herself on that ass James. Good, hard, solid cash. Even you, Nora."

The nurse leapt as if she had been stung.

"Me?" It was nearly a shriek.

"We all know Grandpa was the most generous of men. And we've all known for months what was in the will. He told us last Christmas. Remember?"

"I really don't see that you can involve me," Nora said stiffly, "I was only his nurse."

"And will benefit accordingly, like everyone else who worked for him. And he was very fond of you. He said you were a wonderful nurse and a nice girl."

Nora didn't look as though she found the compliment exactly to her taste.

"Roderick, this is nonsense," Rosalie struck in, "It's only a small amount. Just a token of gratitude. No one would murder for that."

Roderick laughed.

"Don't you believe it. Just you ask Inspector Morton."

Nora stood up.

"I think," she said icily, "that I have had enough of this."

Roderick stretched out a hand and pulled her down on to the arm of his chair.

"Come off it, Nora. I'm only joking."

She gazed down at him doubtfully, but made no move to escape from his grasp.

"I'm only trying to get Marion to snap out of her blues. Anyone can see that she's expecting to be hauled off to prison at a moment's notice. That, and I'm trying to spread the warning. The copper will be after all of us. There's nothing to say that there is only one person at the back of all this. Two would make it that much easier. Which widens the field considerably. Any one of us could have an accomplice in London, doing all the dirty work while we sit safely in Astonley, looking innocent. Or we could divide the work, taking turns to go to London. Mother, you and Marion and I were in Town last Thursday for the inquest. Nora was here. Where were you, David?"

David made a play of lighting his pipe.

"I went to Shrewsbury that day," he replied at last.

"Can you prove it?"

David frowned.

"Don't be an ass."

"Working backwards," Roderick continued, "what about June the second? A Saturday. Your weekend off, Nora.

Marion was in London. Mother was here, as far as I know. I was in Derbyshire."

He looked invitingly at David.

"I went to Bristol to see my sister."

"Which covers the lot of us, once more. But I wonder how well our alibis would stand up to investigation? And the beginning of May, the start of the whole thing? How about that?"

"Rod, this is crazy," David burst out, in exasperation, "What are you trying to prove? That one of us four is a murderer?"

Roderick shrugged.

"Somebody killed James and Alice and Grandpa, didn't they?"

"For heaven's sake leave it to the police."

"We haven't much choice about that," Roderick pointed out, "But I don't see the good of burying our heads in the sand and hoping that they will produce a perfect stranger as the murderer. I don't see how that's possible. I don't say that it is one of us, but it has to be someone who knows quite a lot about us."

"I can't see that it does us any good going into who could have done what," said Rosalie, "Working on your method, Roderick, any of us could be responsible. All we needed was an accommodating friend in London. Which is quite ridiculous. We all have friends in Town, but I can't see myself being able to approach any of mine as accomplices in a complicated series of murders."

"Ah, but it's the money," her son replied, wagging his head at her, "It's the old story. If there's enough money involved, anything can happen."

"You are up to something, Roderick," she said thoughtfully, "I find your concern for Marion touching, but it doesn't ring true. But whatever it is you are plotting, I for one do not intend to help you. And, to bring this intolerable discussion to an end, let me remind you that the police already know where we all were on May the third. You were here, David was here. Marion was in London. So was I. And Nora had taken three days of her holiday. Now, let that be the finish. We shall be going into dinner at any moment and I want to eat it in peace."

It was a vain hope. Even as she spoke, a police car drew up at the front door. From it emerged a weary Inspector Morton and a large bouncing ball of a man, fresh as a daisy after the long soothing train journey from London.

Superintendent Beech.

CHAPTER 8

NO ONE—not even his worst enemy, and there were quite a few people queueing up for the honour of that title—could have accused Reginald Beech of idleness. He was a highly successful detective and over the years had evolved a technique which rarely let him down. Viewed from outside, it appeared to be a frenzy of relentless activity, in all directions, until something—or someone—burst under the pressure. His underlings, groaning and sweating, recognised that there was method in the furious onslaught. And the gaols were full of evildoers who could thank Superintendent Beech for their plight.

Beech had attacked the Winter case with his usual energy, concentrating on the London end of it. He was not pleased with the results. James and Alice Winter had been dead a fortnight, and, in spite of all the hard work, Beech was no further forward than on the day when he had been summoned to the scene of the crime.

"An amateur!" he snorted, as the car bore him smoothly from the station in the little Shropshire town of Oldchurch, "An amateur. But even they know enough nowadays to wear gloves. I've never seen a worse bungle. You'd have thought half the neighbourhood would have heard them breaking into Winter's place. But not a bit of it. Not a single solitary witness have we turned up who saw anyone acting strangely in the vicinity of that house on that Saturday. Keep themselves to themselves, they do, round there," he added, with a final snort.

Inspector Morton maintained a diplomatic silence. He knew by past, and bitter, experience that Superintendent Beech could be a very difficult man.

"I don't believe in hanging around in a murder inquiry, Inspector, as you will no doubt remember," he went on, "It's high time that this case was wrapped up. You got that search warrant?"

"Yes, sir. But—" Morton hesitated, uncertain how best to make his point.

"Well? But what?"

"I don't see that there can be anything to find, sir."

Beech laughed.

"Neither do I, at the moment. But you never know. Murderers keep the oddest things, particularly in a case like this, where the emotions are involved."

Once again Morton hesitated. This was going to be sticky. Then, with an inward sigh, he made up his mind. His own pride in his job forced him to speak.

"You don't feel that the telegram and its consequences have put a different complexion on the matter?" he suggested.

Beech shot him a sharp glance.

"No, I don't, Inspector. If anything, that telegram clinches it."

"It was the death of Robert Winter."

"Pure chance. No one could have forecast that."

"There's a lot of money involved, one way and another."

"I'll grant you that. But it's a pretty chancy method of murdering for gain. It might work and it might not. No, that was spite, Inspector. Pure, unadulterated spite. And further," he went on, in the manner of one demolishing arguments which would be beneath his notice but for his magnanimity, "Suppose that telegram was intended to kill, where does that get you? I know a lot of people benefit under old Winter's will but if it was one of them, what good did James Winter's death do? I gather the old man was fond of his grandson—blind to all his faults, so I'm told—but don't tell me that double murder was committed solely for the purpose of finishing off the old man. Not that it did. He survived that shock somehow."

"Astonley is a very fine property."

"I don't care if it's Buckingham Palace," Beech retorted, "I don't believe it figures in this at all, except on the sidelines. So you've your eye on the heir, have you, Morton? Let me tell you you're wasting your time. I've checked that fellow out. He's been in America for the last three months, all right."

"Everyone at Astonley thought young Roderick was the heir."

"So that's your line of thinking?"

Morton shrugged.

"It's a possibility, sir. But the snag is he would have needed help. He couldn't have done it alone."

"Too fancy," said Beech, "Tell me, have you any particle of evidence against Roderick Winter?"

Morton had to admit that he had not.

"You can forget Roderick Winter," Beech went on, confidently, "You can forget the lot of them. I know it's tempting when there's that much money involved, but I've no doubt that she was counting on us being blinded by it. No, the root of this is hatred. It comes out in every line of that letter. And in that telegram too. It's all centred on James Winter. I've been through his acquaintances with a fine toothcomb. Some liked him, some didn't. But no strong emotions involved, either way. Except for that girl."

Morton did not try to argue further. Beech had made up his mind. They would have to wait and see.

"She didn't impress me much when I saw her in London," Beech was saying, "Lying her head off, or I'm a Dutchman. But she thought that she had got away with it. I'm going to give her a nasty surprise tonight. How far is it now?"

"We're just coming into Winsmere now, sir. Astonley is a mile or so up the road."

The driver slowed to pass through the narrow lanes of the village.

"Pretty," murmured Beech grudgingly, "if you like living in the country, that is."

"We will be there in a few moments, sir. By the way, the family lawyer, name of Walters, arrived this afternoon. I imagine he is staying in the house."

Beech grinned.

"I remember him. I don't think we shall find that he gets in our way at all."

Afterwards, Morton thought that Superintendent Beech must have timed the whole operation carefully, selecting a particular train, to bring him into Shropshire at just the right time, so that he could rush straight to Astonley and catch them unawares. If he had, the plan worked perfectly. The inhabitants of Astonley, stricken and worn down by the day's events, were in no condition to withstand a battering from Beech.

And, as far as Mr Walters was concerned, Beech certainly knew his man. The old lawyer, pleading the fatigue of the journey, had already retired for the night, and was tucking into a large meal brought to him on a tray in his very comfortable bedroom. The arrival of the police perturbed him not at all. He sent a calming message down to an alarmed Rosalic, and begged her not to disturb him unless absolutely necessary.

Rosalie was anything but calmed. The arrival of this man from Scotland Yard, whom instinct had told her was an enemy, from the first moment of her interview with him in London ten days previously, had unnerved her.

"Honestly, Aunt Rosalie," Marion assured her, wanly,

"I'm all right. He can't do anything to me. He has to ask his questions."

She herself was not afraid of Superintendent Beech. He had seemed quite mild and friendly when he talked to her before, when they all went to London the day after James and his poor wife had died. If anything, she was more in awe of Inspector Morton, and was glad that he was not going to ask the questions. She went into the study quite cheerfully, for what she hoped would be the final interview.

Ten minutes later she was in tears, but it seemed that nothing could stem the flood of questions hammering at her ears. Always the same questions, twisted this way and that, but forever bringing the same answers. Somehow or other, Marion managed to choke out her constant denials, unaware that her sobs and protests could be heard clearly by an appalled group gathered in the hall under the watchful eye of a constable. Unaware, too, that a vanload of police had arrived and were meticulously searching every inch of the beautiful house.

Someone tapped at the door, and Beech broke off in mid-sentence. Marion did not look up, thankful only for the moment's respite. She heard Beech heave himself up out of the chair behind Uncle Robert's desk. Then he was standing beside her, thrusting—of all things!—a newspaper under her nose.

"This has just been found in your room, Miss Loring. Take a good look at it, please."

It meant nothing to her. Slowly her head came up, and she stared at him bemused.

"Shaken you, hasn't it?" he said with satisfaction, "You didn't think to get rid of it. Perhaps you thought you might need to write another anonymous letter, and next time it might not be so easy to get hold of a London evening paper to cut the words from. So you kept this one."

"I don't understand," she said faintly.

"Don't try to kid me," he scoffed, "You understand well enough. This," he shook the newspaper in front of her face, "this is part of a copy of a London evening newspaper dated 2nd May. The day before that anonymous letter was sent to Mr Winter. And the words which made up that letter were all cut from a copy of that particular newspaper. Now, you were in London on May the second and on the next day. So what about it? And let's have the truth this time."

"But that's not my newspaper."

"It was found in your room. Under the bed, where you had hidden it."

"But that's impossible." Suddenly, through the confusion of her mind, came the explanation. "I remember now. I found it in Nurse Deeping's room. I must have carried it away by mistake. It dropped under the bed when I went into my room to find a safety pin. Tonight."

The hard face was a study in disbelief.

"Fetch me the Deeping woman," he said, after a long moment.

Inspector Morton himself slipped out of the room on the errand.

Nora came in, cool and collected as usual, but unsmiling.

"This yours?" demanded Beech, proffering the newspaper.

Nora looked at it and shrugged.

"I've no idea. It's an old one. Why?"

"She," Beech jerked his head in Marion's direction, "says she picked it up in your room. Tonight."

Nora's eyebrows rose.

"If Marion says so, then it must be so. There is a pile of newspapers in my room. I was sorting out my things earlier on."

Beech favoured her with a long stare.

"You were in London at the beginning of May?"

She stared back at him, unconcerned.

"You know I was. The police here took statements from all of us over that business of the letter. My family home is there, and I was spending a few days' holiday with them."

"Do you buy evening papers?"

"Sometimes."

"Did you then?"

"I don't remember. Probably."

"And why would you keep one?"

Nora shrugged.

"To wrap something in."

"All right," said Beech sourly, "I'll see you again later. You can go."

Nora glanced speculatively at Marion, opened her mouth to speak, then changed her mind. Without another word, she hurried from the room.

Inspector Morton returned.

"The housemaid insists there was no newspaper under Miss Loring's bed when she did the room yesterday, sir," he said quietly.

Beech glanced at him briefly.

"Very efficient of you, Inspector," he said, ominously. He turned back to Marion. "I am taking you into Oldchurch, Miss Loring, to the police station there. I am not satisfied with your statements and I propose to go over them with you until I am satisfied. Constable!"

The shout brought the man from the hall, running.

"Sir?"

"Take Miss Loring out to the car, please. And stay with her." He watched balefully while Marion was led away. He heard a commotion start up outside in the hall. He thrust out a hand to slam the door shut. "It will be a long session, Inspector. But I'll get the truth out of her eventually."

"There's not enough evidence to hold her, sir."

Beech laughed.

"At the moment there's none at all. But she doesn't know that. It's a confession I'm after."

Superintendent Beech stamped out of the room in the wake of his prey. The clamour in the hall ceased abruptly and Morton, hanging back in the study, heard his superior's voice laying down the law to whoever was out there.

It was in that moment that he gave in to his growing conviction that Marion Loring was innocent. He hoped that he was not prompted by personal animosity towards Beech.

Reluctantly he went out into the hall. Keeping Beech waiting would do no good at all. He was wondering what he could do to help the girl. The matter was out of his hands.

Beech's bulky figure was blocking out the light in the porch. Morton saw the Superintendent check his stride, and stiffen.

"What the—!" he exclaimed, and stopped.

Then he lumbered forward to a strange car which had just pulled up behind the police van. He reached it as Charles Warren emerged from behind the wheel.

"What the hell are you doing here?"

Morton did not attend to the unruffled reply. It was the first time that he had seen Beech shaken out of his complacency. It had given him a bright idea.

CHAPTER 9

It was many hours before Marion returned to Astonley. Beech questioned her far into the night, until even he threw in his hand and left her to rest. By morning he was at the attack once more. Marion, dizzy with fatigue, for the few hours' respite had not brought her sleep, gazed up into the harsh face and wondered how she could last the day.

There was nothing she could do. Only endure. She could not confess to a crime which she had not committed.

"What I want to know," thundered Beech, "is what happened during James Winter's visit to his old home at the end of April. Don't pretend that nothing happened. I know damned well that something did."

Marion shook her head. No one except she and James knew what had taken place between them. And James was dead. She had confided in no one.

"James Winter spent a week at Astonley," Beech was saying, "He was alone. His wife wasn't with him. For the first time since his marriage. He was there for a week; in fact he was still there on the day when the anonymous letter turned up. But you weren't. You had gone off to London on the first of May. Unexpectedly. That letter turned up on the third. You came back to Astonley on the fourth, sent for by Mr Robert Winter. And on the sixth you started writing after jobs away from Astonley. Again unexpectedly. So, what made you do it?"

Marion remained silent. The truth would not benefit her. Nor would lies.

From his position behind the Superintendent, Inspector Morton was willing her to answer. It was obvious that she was holding something back. She was only making the situation worse for herself.

"We have a witness who saw you and James Winter together in the garden," Beech reminded her.

Marion thought: Mrs Lightfoot: it must be; she was always prowling round after James.

Beech smashed his clenched fist down on the desk.

"Answer me!"

But, in spite of Morton's attempts at telepathy, Marion was stubbornly silent.

"James and Alice Winter were poisoned by arsenic," Beech changed the direction of his questioning suddenly. "Not pure arsenic, but an ordinary commercial preparation for use in the garden. There's a tin of it in the potting shed at Astonley. Half-full. And plenty of fingerprints on it. Including yours. Explain that."

"I have done. Several times," Marion replied doggedly, "I told you I was using it. For the normal purpose. Pest destroying."

"Why you? There's a gardener."

"I like gardening."

Beech snorted in derision. He might almost have been that curmudgeonly old gardener himself, who didn't hold with anyone messing about in his domain. To keep the peace, Robert Winter had had to give Marion a patch all to herself. Even so, it was still a source of trouble. The more her little garden blossomed under her hands, the more it enraged the gardener.

And so it went on, all through that long Sunday morning. . . .

At last Mr Walters arrived, his old eyes snapping with the excitement. Marion recoiled from him. She had never been more afraid of him in her life.

But there was another man with him, tall, dark, authoritative. A stranger, whose quiet voice reassured her. She had no idea who he was, but suddenly, illogically, she recognised a friend.

His arrival seemed to upset Superintendent Beech. For the moment Marion herself was forgotten as he turned to face this new and unwelcome antagonist. She was shepherded away into another room and left alone for a long time.

Beech himself came to her, his face like thunder.

"I'm sending you home," he announced. "But don't imagine that I have done with you." He paused and stared at her. "I never give up," he added softly.

Marion hardly took in the words. Beech's venom was wasted. She did not understand that she was free to go until she found herself standing on the steps of the police station, smelling the fresh, sweet air.

The street was almost deserted, quiet under the blessed calm of a summer Sunday. A small group of people stood on the pavement, two cars waited at the kerb. As Marion emerged from the building, old Mr Walters was climbing into the front car. With a word to those remaining behind, but not a glance towards the girl hesitating in the doorway, he settled himself and directed the driver to be off.

Marion stared down at the three people at the foot of the steps. The stranger was there, and Sir John Prout and a girl she recognised as his grand-daughter.

Hope Warren turned her head and caught sight of her. "Marion!" She held out her hands.

The girl ran to her.

Hope hugged her.

"It's all right, Marion. Don't cry."

But for a moment, Marion sobbed in the older girl's arms.

Sir John was busy opening the doors of the car.

"Come on," he said briskly, "No point in hanging about

here. Marion, child, in you get. We're taking you home."

He hustled the girls into the back seat, while he ran round to the front passenger seat.

"Hurry up, Charles," he said urgently, "Drive us back home. That fellow might change his mind."

Charles Warren laughed, but obediently took the driving seat and started the engine.

"Superintendent Beech doesn't waste his time in fighting hopeless battles," he said as they passed through the silent little town.

"I don't understand," Marion said faintly, "How did you manage to get me out of there?"

"Charles did it," Sir John informed her proudly.

Hope laughed suddenly.

"Poor Marion! She doesn't even know who Charles is." She turned to the girl. "It's a bit late for introductions. Charles is my husband."

"I should have guessed," Marion murmured, "But how did he manage to get me out?"

"I didn't," said Charles, "Mr Walters persuaded Superintendent Beech that if he didn't intend to charge you he should let you go."

"Mr Walters!" Marion exclaimed, "That horrible old man! Last night he wouldn't raise a finger to help me."

"Nor would he have done today," said Sir John shortly, "If Charles hadn't put a bit of pressure on him."

"Oh," Marion could not imagine Mr Walters giving way under any sort of pressure, but the fact remained that she was out of that terrible place and on her way back to Astonley. "I don't know how you did it," she said frankly, "but I'm very thankful that you did. But what will happen now?"

There was a silence in the car.

"I'm afraid you must expect further trouble," Charles said evenly after a while, "Superintendent Beech doesn't give up. Clearly he hasn't enough evidence to hold you or we should never have been able to get you out of there. But he will go on looking."

"But he can't find something that isn't there," Marion protested.

Back in the police station in Oldchurch, Beech was fuming. The word had run round, and everyone who could was keeping out of his way. Inspector Morton, philosophically accepting his lot, bore the brunt of it.

"That little bitch needn't think she is going to get away with this," Beech growled, "There must be some evidence somewhere."

"What about the post office where that telegram was handed in?" suggested Morton.

Beech snorted.

"Stupid clot! No, I don't mean you, Inspector. I'm referring to that snotty little clerk who took in the telegram. Name of Price. Bloody Welshman. Looked down his nose at me and told me he couldn't possibly remember who had handed the thing in. Far too many people sending telegrams all the time. No, that's no good. The only hope is the break-in at Winter's place. If I could just find one witness who could place the Loring girl near that house. . . ."

At Astonley, Marion slept, soothed by a tablet administered by Nora Deeping.

Downstairs there was a lively discussion in progress. In the course of it old quarrels were reappearing and old scores being paid off.

"Robert Winter was a fool," Mr Walters proclaimed acidly, "I warned him many a time that a man in his position must beware of hangers-on. But he wouldn't listen to me. He insisted on taking in that child, though she had no sort of claim on him. Godfather, indeed! Who cares about things like that nowadays? But that was Robert all over. And Marion isn't the only hanger-on here. What did James Winter do for his keep? Or you, Roderick? What do you do?"

Rosalie, appalled, yet hopelessly involved, was thinking that such a thing would never have been said in this house a week ago. Clearly, Mr Walters had held these opinions for many years, but he had never voiced them in public before. And in front of virtual strangers, too! She glanced worriedly at the Warrens. Grateful though she was to them for what they had done for Marion, yet she wished they would go.

"Rubbish!" exclaimed Sir John loudly.

Mr Walters glared malevolently at him.

"And what do you know about it, sir?"

"Plenty. Quite a lot more than you do, let me tell you. Robert was my friend all his life. He liked having these young people round him. He would have been very lonely without them. They made him happy. I don't call that sponging."

"That girl should be sent packing," Mr Walters went on, addressing himself to Rosalie and ignoring Sir John. "There is no reason for her to stay on here now that Robert is dead. Quite unsuitable, too, since Mr Thomas Winter is unmarried."

"I shall be here," said Rosalie coldly.

"Ha! I thought so!" Mr Walters said with satisfaction, "I didn't think you would be moving back into the Dower House until you were forced. I noticed you moved up here quickly enough last week. I shall advise the heir that he is under no obligation to support you. The Dower House could be let profitably."

Roderick jumped to his feet, his face white with anger.

Hope Warren, who had been sending meaning looks at her menfolk for the past ten minutes, also leapt up, made the briefest of farewells and swept her husband and her grandfather out of the house, leaving the family to fight it out.

Marion slept the clock round. She woke to bright sun shining through the curtains. A glance at the clock over the mantelpiece told her that it was five o'clock. It had been three before she had crept into bed, and she knew that she had slept more than two hours. It must be Monday.

For a while she lay quietly, enjoying the peace. There was no sound of movement in the house, but at this time of the day, late afternoon, it was nothing unusual for Astonley to be wrapped in silence. It was as if time had been pushed back, to the days before violence and hatred had entered their lives.

Presently she got up, bathed and dressed. The events of the past few days seemed remote and unreal. It was difficult to believe that they had happened at all.

A brisk fantasia on a motor horn at the front of the house broke her dream.

At once the place came to life and there were footsteps in the hall.

It's Superintendent Beech, thought Marion in a panic; he's come back for me.

But she ran downstairs all the same.

A total stranger was standing in the middle of the hall, gazing round at the ancient furniture and the time-darkened portraits lining the walls. Bars of bright light from the long mullioned windows picked out hands and faces, and here and there a fold of rich cloth, from the canvases.

"Wow!" he breathed, and there was a hint of an accent in his voice. "So this is Astonley."

He was of middle height, brown-haired; perhaps in his late twenties. An ordinary, undistinguished little man, Marion decided.

He turned and saw her, hesitating at the foot of the staircase.

He smiled, a pleasant smile, which lit up his whole face. He stepped forward, his hand outstretched.

"I'm Thomas Winter," he announced.

CHAPTER 10

WITH the arrival of Thomas, everything changed. The police bothered them no more. Inspector Morton made a brief appearance at the funeral, but faded away discreetly afterwards. Superintendent Beech had gone back to London. So had Mr Walters, nursing his spite. Friends and neighbours called, and life suddenly swung back into its accustomed routine. By Thursday morning, Astonley was itself again.

Marion, armed with a bunch of catalogues of farm machinery, headed for the land agent's office with a lighter heart. Even the weather was favouring them, she thought, for the unusually long spell of brilliant weather still showed no signs of breaking.

David was in his office. He looked up at Marion's entrance, his face unsmiling.

"Tom asked me to bring these back to you," she said, laying down her burden on the top of the nearest filing cabinet, "He says he found them very interesting and will go through them with you one day next week."

"Thanks."

The brusqueness dampened her spirits.

"He's really trying very hard, you know. He's mad keen on the estate, and he wants to learn."

David's face softened a little.

"He's won you over I see."

Marion smiled.

"It's a bit pathetic, David. He wants to be one of us so much. And he's not a bit what we feared. He's not brash or pushing. And he's been very kind to me. After all, I'm not a relative. I've no claim on him. But he's told me he'd be glad if I would stay on for as long as I feel I can. He says I will be a help to him with our neighbours." She glanced away, unable to meet David's suddenly questioning look. "It's not true. Aunt Rosalie is in a better position for that. Tom has asked her to move up from the Dower House for a while, to act as his hostess until he has settled in, and she's agreed. So you see, I shan't be earning my keep. But it's good of him to let me stay on until I find a suitable job."

"What are you going to do?"

Marion shrugged.

"What I'm trained for. Secretarial work. In London, I think. If I had the courage of my convictions, I would get on the next train and install myself in some hostel and find work at once."

"And why don't you?"

Marion turned sharply to stare at him. The harsh tone was so unlike the David she had known for so many years. Bitterly she told herself that she ought not to be surprised at it nor lulled into imagining that life had returned to normal. The truth was that nothing would ever be the same again. People whom she had taken for granted had turned into strangers. Perhaps it was that now she was seeing them as they really were and for the first time.

"I don't want to leave Astonley," she blurted out the truth, and rushed on, "I ought to have made the break immediately, but that would have meant telling Uncle Robert what had happened. I couldn't do that. It would have hurt him too much. I thought it would be easier if I did the thing gradually. So I pretended I'd got tired of living in the country. He didn't try to stop me. He let me dash off to London, at a moment's notice. It didn't occur to me at the time, but I think he must have guessed—something. So I—" She stopped, suddenly aware that her tongue had run away with her. "David, forget it. I must be getting back."

But he barred her passage, his face stern.

"Marion, I want the truth. What did James do to you when he was here last April?"

He put his hands on her shoulders.

She stared up into his face, not at all reassured by what she saw.

"You have already let out enough for me to make a few guesses," he went on, "But I would rather you told me yourself."

She pressed her lips together firmly, wondering how she could have been so stupid to have burst out like that. She had resolved that she would tell no one. She could hardly bear to think, let alone *talk*, about it.

The pressure on her shoulders increased cruelly.

"You're hurting me," she gasped.

David ignored the appeal.

"I want the truth, Marion," he repeated.

How he had changed! From the mainstay and support of her childhood, into this demanding inquisitor! But there was an authority about him which roused some chord in her. She wished she could obey him, could pour out the whole miserable story.

But it wouldn't do. This was a burden she had to carry alone.

"Nothing happened," she said, as steadily as she could, "Except that I realised what a fool I had been." At least, that was the literal truth. "I realised that I must make a life for myself—away from here," she added.

David was reluctant to accept the explanation, but the pressure of his hands on her shoulders relaxed.

Marion seized the opportunity to escape from him. She dodged out of his reach.

"You can understand why I was reluctant to leave Astonley," she went on, with an attempt at lightness, "And Uncle Robert, too. After all, it has been my home for so long. And I haven't any family of my own."

"You will find it lonely in London."

"I have some friends there. Girls whom I was at school with. And I am sure to meet some new people."

"All the same, you will have to live alone," he pointed out.

"I shall manage. Thousands, millions of others do."

He wandered back to his desk. He stood there, looking down at a pile of correspondence.

"You don't have to leave Astonley, Marion."

She stared at him.

"But David, I can't sponge on Tom indefinitely. And there would be no suitable work for me round here. Uncle Robert has left me some money, but I couldn't afford to do nothing."

"You could marry me," he said curtly.

Marion could not believe her ears.

"Marry you?" she faltered.

"I can't offer you Astonley, but we could be quite comfortable here."

He means it! she thought wonderingly.

"I'm not asking you to fall in love with me, Marion," he went on, still not looking directly at her, "Liking is quite enough to build a marriage on."

It was a good offer, and, to the astonished girl, as cold as charity.

"Thank you, David," she said at last, "but it wouldn't work."

"As you please," he returned politely. He picked up a bundle of papers. "Would you mind giving these to Tom? I'm rather busy this morning to go up to the house."

Plainly it was a dismissal. Marion was thankful to him for allowing her to escape from an embarrassing situation so quickly. It would be different, she told herself, as she walked swiftly up the path to Astonley, if David were in love with her. Then she would have to avoid him, to save his feelings. But there was no love involved on either side. He had offered her a home out of kindness. Her refusal would not disturb their relationship.

As she approached the garden gate a voice hailed her.

"Hi, there, Marion!"

Tom was standing on the terrace. Now he came strolling across the lawn to meet her.

"I was wondering where you had disappeared to."

"I took those catalogues back to David." She held out the papers which David had given to her. "And I've brought these back for you to look at."

He took them from her and flipped through them.

"Come into the study and help me with them. Anyway, there's a job we have to do."

"What's that?"

"Write out an advertisement for a new housekeeper," he grinned.

"Oh," Marion gasped, "Mrs Lightfoot's going?"

"She is. At the end of the month," his grin broadened, "I've given her the boot."

Marion felt herself colour.

"Not on my account I hope?"

Tom checked his stride and turned to look straight at her.

"Entirely on your account, Marion. Rosalie has been putting me in the picture."

Her cheeks were burning now.

"But, Tom, you shouldn't. Mrs Lightfoot is a very good housekeeper. And I shall be going away soon."

"I hope you'll change your mind about that," he replied softly, "That Lightfoot woman won't alter her opinions about you, and that means there is no place for her in my house."

There was open admiration in his eyes.

Marion looked away, unable to meet the challenge.

"It's very good of you, Tom," she said unsteadily.

"I mean it."

"I wish the police shared your confidence in me."

"They must be crazy to think that you could have done that. And don't you bother your head any more about them. They will have to reckon with me if they come sniffing after you again."

Marion had to laugh. It was all nonsense. Superintendent Beech could not be scared off by anyone. But it was a comfort to have a champion.

There was something rather nice about Thomas Winter, she decided.

On the terrace, Tom halted.

"Marion," he said softly, and she too stood still, "You're a real English rose, you are."

"The post has come," announced a voice behind her.

Marion swung round. Roderick, a bundle of letters in his hand, was standing in the hall. His face wore an ironic smile and she guessed that he had heard Tom's remark, through the open doors to the terrace. She felt the colour rush up into her cheeks.

"Letter for you, Marion," Roderick went on, "And one for you, Tom." He scrutinized the envelope before handing it over. "From Bristol."

"Well, I've lived there for the past six years," said Tom easily, taking the letter and putting it with the other papers he was carrying. "If it is of any interest to you."

Roderick glared at him.

"None at all, I assure you," he snapped, and left them.

Marion gazed after him.

"I'm sorry, Tom. Roderick is behaving very badly. Don't take any notice of him."

Tom laughed.

"He'll get used to it. Not that I can blame him," he said frankly, "In his position I would be as sore as a boil. Imagine thinking you had inherited this lot, only to have it snatched from under your nose."

They went into the study.

"Half a tick," said Tom, "I'll just have a squint at my letter before we start."

He tore open the envelope.

It was two or three moments before Marion realised that something was wrong. She looked up to see Tom standing absolutely still, the letter in his hand, his face rigid.

"Why, Tom, what is the matter?"

Immediately he relaxed.

"I'm sorry, Marion." He stuffed the letter into his pocket. "I'm afraid these papers of David's will have to wait."

"Is it bad news?" she asked anxiously.

"Well, yes, it is." He passed his hand over his eyes. "It takes a bit of getting used to." He sighed. "It's my old cousin, Maud. My mother's cousin, really. She took me in, when I came over here. I haven't seen much of her these past couple of years. I ought to have done. Now the old soul's dead. Road accident."

"I'm so sorry."

"So am I. Particularly since I'd neglected her a bit. That's the way of things. I'll have to go to Bristol right away. It's the least I can do."

Half an hour later, his bag hastily packed, Thomas Winter was on his way. Marion stood in the drive, watching his car disappear round the first curve.

Tom would not be away long, but, even so, she was going to miss him.

CHAPTER 11

INSPECTOR MORTON hesitated on the steps of the large, ugly building fronting on Whitehall. Once he went through that door, he would have committed himself.

But he was already committed—to opposing Superintendent Beech, and to succeed he needed to use every weapon which came to hand. He would have to present a more than watertight case to convince Beech.

The doorman took his name, wrote it down on a slip of paper, and withdrew into his office to do some telephoning, while Morton kicked his heels. A few moments later a messenger appeared to conduct the Inspector upstairs. Even the police weren't allowed to wander freely about the Ministry of Security.

Resolutely, Morton banished doubts from his mind. And hadn't Beech himself presented him with this opportunity, by summoning him to a meeting in London this Friday morning?

He was ushered into Charles Warren's office.

"Inspector! This is a welcome surprise. I didn't know you were in Town."

Morton accepted the proffered hand, then the chair which Charles pulled forward.

"I came for a meeting, Mr Warren. So I thought I would call."

"I'm glad to see you. How is the Astonley affair going? Or can't you tell me?"

Morton relaxed and grinned.

"I don't need to play games with you, Mr Warren. I am hoping you might be able to help me."

"What's bothering you, Inspector? Superintendent Beech?"

Morton laughed outright.

"You can say that again. But I don't need to tell you anything about him, I gather."

"You don't," Charles replied, with an answering grin, "I won't bore you with the details, but the good Superintendent and I had an encounter a little while back. We did not see eye to eye."

"Judging by some of the remarks he made about you in Oldchurch last Sunday, I shouldn't think you did. But he was so sore at you, you must have got the better of him."

Charles shook his head.

"No, I would call it a draw. I must admit, I don't feel honour was satisfied. Neither does he, I imagine. What's your trouble with him?"

Morton's smile vanished.

"He's after Marion Loring. I don't agree with him."

"No?"

"She's not helping herself by lying about James Winter's visit to Astonley at the end of April. She doesn't seem to understand that, no matter what it was that happened, or however much she doesn't want to talk about it, lying only creates the impression that the rest of her evidence can't be believed. And, also, it leaves her without an explanation for why she suddenly decided to leave home and get a job in London."

Charles frowned.

"There must be a strong reason for her to keep it back. My wife says that she is an intelligent girl. She must realise that she is putting herself into an unfortunate position."

"I'm sure I've pointed it out to her enough," agreed Morton unhappily, "Beech says it is because the truth would underline her guilt. But I don't see it. Any explanation would be better than offering none. As it is, we are left with the housekeeper's evidence. She saw them together and from what she saw came to the conclusion that Marion had been trying to get James Winter back—and had failed. But even Beech doesn't want to use her as the sole witness," Morton added, "Any barrister worth his salt could persuade a jury that Mrs Lightfoot had made up the whole story out of sheer spite."

"And has she?"

"On balance, I'd say no. She may have misinterpreted what she saw, but I'm convinced that she did see something. But if only Marion Loring would come clean, I know which one of the two I would rather believe."

"You believe everything else Marion says?"

Morton nodded.

"I'm inclined to. Of course, I might be wrong. Murderers come in all sorts and sizes. And you can make out a motive for her. A woman scorned and all that. Not to mention the fact that it must be a bit of a come-down to be looking for a job as a shorthand-typist when you've been expecting to be mistress of a house like Astonley."

"That's what is bothering you, isn't it?" asked Charles shrewdly, "Astonley."

"Yes. When you get murders with that much money lying around, it must figure in the crime somewhere."

"So who do you fancy?"

"Roderick Winter is my bet. They all thought he was the heir. No one knew a thing about Thomas, except old Robert Winter and his lawyer. And didn't old man Walters get a kick out of springing the glad tidings on the family! You can be sure he hadn't let out a word about it before Robert Winter died."

"And could Roderick have done the murders?"

Morton sighed.

"That's the whole point. He couldn't have done them without an accomplice. That is true of everyone in the family, except Marion Loring. And I don't think she is the one. So it has to be one of the others. And Roderick was the one who expected to inherit the estate."

"An accomplice," echoed Charles thoughtfully, "Someone at Astonley?"

"Not necessarily. It could be a friend in London."

"A good friend, who will break into someone's house and stir arsenic into the food."

"He wouldn't have had to do that. Roderick himself could have fixed that. He was away from Astonley that weekend. He went over to Derbyshire, where he had borrowed a cottage from a pal of his."

"Oh?" said Charles, interested, "And was this pal there with him?"

"He was not. Roderick collected the key from him on the Friday night, and took it back on Monday morning. This friend lives near Manchester. Now the cottage is in a pretty wild part of the Peak District. I had the local police poke around a bit. Roderick's car was seen there on Friday night, and again on Sunday morning. But for the rest of the time he could have been anywhere in the world. We don't know at what time the break-in at James Winter's place took place. Could have been anytime that weekend. Roderick Winter could have driven to London and back to that cottage without anyone being the wiser."

"And what about the other things? The letter and the telegram."

"He could have sent the telegram. He was in Town that day, for the inquest, with his mother and Miss Loring. But he couldn't have sent that letter off himself. I suppose he could have prepared it, if he had had the foresight to provide himself with a London evening newspaper, which certainly is never on sale in Shropshire. But someone else would have had to mail it for him."

"The accomplice, in fact."

"That's right, Mr Warren. And the devil of it is that the accomplice might have had no idea what it was that he was posting. Just an envelope with a typed address. And Roderick could have explained the whole thing by saying it was a joke he was playing on his grandfather."

"But surely that person would come forward now? There has been enough in the Press about the anonymous letter."

"They might not have connected the two up," Morton replied gloomily.

"What about the envelope? You said it was typed. Can it be traced to a machine at Astonley? I expect there is one."

"Two, in fact. One in the house and one in the Land Agent's office. But neither of those was used for that envelope. But what does that prove, for heaven's sake?"

"Nothing," Charles agreed ruefully. "There are plenty of typewriters about. I see what you are up against, Inspector. What do you want me to do?"

"Just one thing, Mr Warren. I can tackle his friends myself. But there is one person I can't get at, not without treading on Superintendent Beech's toes."

"And who is that?"

"The clerk in the post office who took in the telegram. One Benjamin Price. He told Beech that he couldn't remember who had handed the thing in. Perhaps he didn't try very hard."

Charles nodded.

"You've a point there, Inspector. It's amazing what people can remember if they go about it the right way. All right, I'll have a go at him for you. Have you a photograph of Roderick I can use?"

Morton fished an envelope out of his pocket and laid it on the desk.

"There you are. I'll be going now, Mr Warren. And thank you."

Charles laughed.

"I haven't done anything yet. I'll be in touch."

Morton paused at the door.

"There's only one thing, Mr Warren. Time might be running short. Beech has found a rag-and-bone man who says he saw a blonde girl near James Winter's house on the afternoon of Saturday May the second. Beech thinks it must have been Marion Loring. Fortunately for her, the man couldn't be sure about his description—but it might be different if he saw her in a line-up."

Unexpectedly, the day had dragged for Marion. There was no one about the house. Rosalie had carried off her reluctant son to a teaparty with a neighbour whom Roderick complained was a bore. Nora Deeping, her things packed ready for her departure from Astonley on the morrow, had gone into Oldchurch to settle the final arrangements for the transport of her heavy luggage. Mrs Lightfoot was sure to be somewhere in the house, but Marion had no desire for her company.

Not that she wanted company. She was quite happy on her own. Yet the hours seemed long.

Idiot! she told herself at last. You're waiting for Tom to come home.

It had been so long since she had had someone to wait for. . . .

He came late that night, just when she had abandoned hope. She heard the car and ran to meet him with a speed and lightness which brought questioning glances from Roderick and his mother.

But Tom himself was a disappointment. He looked tired and depressed, his usual cheerfulness gone.

"What a day!" he sighed, "I don't like funerals. Two in a week is a bit much. But am I glad to be home!"

Marion faded into the background, leaving Rosalie to fuss over Tom, to organise supper for him, to provide him with a drink while it was being prepared. Perhaps she had imagined it all, had sold herself on the idea that Tom might be interested in her just because she was miserable and hurt and lonely. Certainly, he didn't seem overjoyed to see her tonight. But she could not bring herself to creep off quielty to her bedroom. He was tired and hungry. Later it might be different.

It was.

At eleven o'clock, Tom said suddenly, "I've something to tell you."

They looked up, Rosalie from her embroidery, Nora and Roderick from newspapers, Marion from a book of which she had hardly read a word for the past hour.

Tom looked round at the startled faces truculently.

"I'll be having a guest here, in a fortnight's time," he announced, "A lady. Her name is Bella Manston. She is my fiancée."

Marion felt her hands shaking. She took a firm grip on her book. She would be ashamed for anyone to see. And she knew that Roderick's sharp eyes had left Tom to fasten on her.

"That's very nice, Tom," said Rosalie placidly, "Do tell us about her."

She picked up her needle and began to sew again. Marion felt the tension go out of her, though her heart was beating faster than usual and seemed to be up in her throat.

"She's an American," Tom's voice was still taut, aggressive, "I met her on the boat coming over."

"A lightning romance," commented Roderick, and the sneer was unmistakable.

Rosalie shot him a quelling glance.

"I fell in love with your father in a matter of ten minutes," she said calmly, "So she is coming in a fortnight, Tom? Couldn't you bring her here sooner?"

"She's going to Scotland with some friends on Monday. She'll come here as soon as they are back."

"And where is she now?"

Tom was beginning to relax, but still it seemed as if he were expecting trouble.

"In London."

Rosalie smiled at him.

"You must give me her address. I'll write to her tonight, telling her that we shall look forward to meeting her. She will have it by Monday. Where is she staying?"

Tom hesitated.

"I'm not going to write and tell her we don't want her, Tom."

Tom summoned an answering smile.

"I'm sorry, Rosalie. You're being too kind. It's just that Bella is going to find Astonley a bit of a surprise. It's not what she's been used to."

"I'll bet it isn't," muttered Roderick.

The smile left Tom's face abruptly.

"Then all the more reason for me to write to welcome her," Rosalie said quickly, "Do give me the address, Tom."

"Royal View Hotel, Cromwell Road," he said reluctantly, his eyes on Roderick.

Rosalie was hunting in her handbag for her diary. She jotted down the address.

"And it is Miss Bella Manston. Is Bella her proper name?"

"No. Arabella, and it's not Miss. It's Mrs. She's divorced."

"My God!" said Roderick loudly, and stamped out of the room.

He left an awkward silence behind him.

"Tom, I can only say that I am sorry," Rosalie said, breaking it. "I'll speak to Roderick. I'm sure your fiancée is a nice girl, no matter what her background or previous connections. We shall welcome her for your sake."

"Will *he*?"

"Of course. Don't take any notice of Roderick. And he has a fortnight to get used to the idea."

"I was afraid I would run into trouble over this," Tom admitted, "I didn't think you would take it as well as you have, Rosalie. I'm really grateful. I thought I would go away for this fortnight, too. Take the car over to France and have a look round over there. Then I'll collect Bella in London and bring her here. Would that help?"

Rosalie smiled.

"I think that is an excellent idea."

Marion noticed that never once had Tom looked at her. He's forgotten that I exist, she thought. And to think that I imagined that he might be interested in me! Just as well to find out now, when the hurt involved is so small.

But nevertheless, there was a sense of desolation. Later, she stood at her open window, gazing out into the dark garden. She had put out the light in her room, feeling herself at one with the gentle melancholy of the night.

Then she became aware that there was someone below her, on the terrace. Forgetting herself, she leant further out, peering down. One form, then another detached itself from the shadows, came together to form one dark, embracing mass, then set out over the lawn, arms entwined.

Marion stared after them. The moon came out from behind a cloud and shone down on them.

It was Roderick—and Nora Deeping.

CHAPTER 12

NORA was the first person whom Marion saw the following morning. She met her at the head of the stairs as she was on her way down to breakfast. Nora was wearing a suit, in spite of the day's promise of heat.

"Aren't you going to be hot in that?"

Nora shrugged.

"It's easier to wear it than to pack it."

"Of course, you're going. I'd forgotten."

Marion looked at the other girl curiously. It struck her that she knew very little about Nora, although they had lived under the same roof for so many months. The nurse was not one to share confidences. Marion did not even know her exact age, though she guessed it as nearing thirty.

Too old for Roderick.

And not at all his type. Marion had been considerably surprised by what she saw in the garden last night. She had had no inkling of an affair between Roderick and Nora. Quite the reverse. Until last night she had thought that Roderick's interest lay in a girl who lived on the other side of the county. Not a girl whom Marion cared for, but one eminently suited to be connected with Astonley. She wondered how long this affair had been going on.

"Will you miss us?" she asked. It was the nearest to a direct question that she dared go.

Did she imagine that Nora's glance was particularly sharp?

"Will you miss me?" Nora countered smoothly.

It was at that moment that they heard the raised voices. They came from the diningroom, clearly, unmistakably angry. The girls on the staircase stopped and stared at each other in frank consternation.

"Roderick," said Nora faintly.

Marion did not stop to consider that that one word had answered all her questions. She had recognised both the shouting voices. Roderick and Tom were at it, hammer and tongs, and they had to be stopped.

"Come on," she urged, and together they ran down into the hall and across to the diningroom.

Marion flung open the door in time to hear Tom say furiously.

"I've had enough of this. This is my house and I don't intend to let people insult my future wife in here. So you can go. Both of you. If you're so set against Bella now, when you've never even seen her, what is it going to be like when she arrives? So you can get out. Now."

"Look here—" Roderick began angrily, but Tom cut him short.

"*You* look here. I don't have to keep you. You've no claim on me. Old Walters tried to warn me, but I didn't take any notice of him. But he knew a thing or two. I can see that now. So you can go. From here, and from the Dower House. I'm giving you notice."

Then there was silence.

Outside the open door, unnoticed by the quarrelling men, the two girls exchanged glances.

"What shall we do?" whispered Nora.

"We can't go in," Marion whispered back, "Not for a minute."

From where they were they could see neither the table nor the antagonists.

Then Rosalie spoke, and the girls relaxed. Oddly, her presence eased their situation. With a shock, Marion realised that both she and Nora had been fearing violence.

"That is entirely up to you, Tom," she said calmly, "I'm sorry you feel like that, but if you do, then you do. No, Roderick," she went on sternly, "You have already said more than enough. You will please be quiet."

"Let him speak," growled Tom.

"No. It's my turn now," she replied, still refusing to be drawn into quarrelling, "I am quite willing to leave the Dower House. It was my intention anyway. When do you want us to go?"

"Oh, go when you like," he flung back at her.

The girls in the hall heard a chair scrape back and stamping feet. Silently, they fell back. A few seconds later, Tom emerged, his face set. He passed them without seeing them.

They slipped into the room.

Roderick was saying urgently, "Mother! Now look what you've done. He didn't mean that. About giving us notice. It shook him when you accepted it. Now he can't take it back, and nor can you."

"Don't blame me," Rosalie replied coldly, "You started the quarrel." She looked up and saw the girls. "Ah, there you are, Nora. And Marion. Come and have breakfast."

They took their places at the table. Roderick stared gloomily at his plate, while Rosalie, white-faced but composed, tried to pretend that nothing had happened. But her hand shook as she poured coffee for Nora. She stared down at the brown spreading stain on the white tablecloth.

"I'm sorry. I'll ring for some more."

But she made no move towards the bell-push by the fireplace.

"Marion and I heard all that," Nora said quietly.

Roderick looked up quickly. His mother relaxed visibly.

"Then I don't need to explain," she said and her voice was unsteady. For once she looked every year of her age.

"And at breakfast, too! What a time for a quarrel. Now, girls, eat up. We shall have a lot to do, this morning. Nora, what time is your train?"

"Ten-thirty."

"Then you and Roderick had better go into Oldchurch as soon as you have finished your breakfast. You know what the traffic is like there on a Saturday morning. Marion, you will have to come back with me to the Dower House. You can't stay here on your own with Tom."

"No, I suppose not," Marion murmured, "I must look for a job, too."

"So must Roderick," said Rosalie sharply, "I think the best thing we can do is take a flat in London, the three of us. There is no point in you being on your own, Marion. You might as well stay with us. At least we have a fortnight, thank heavens, while Tom is away. It will be a rush, but Marion and I can get everything packed. Roderick, you will have to go to Town next week and find us somewhere to live. That way we can be out of the Dower House by the time Tom brings his fiancée here."

"Mother!" Roderick exclaimed, appalled.

"It's no use," she said firmly, "This is the way it has to be, Roderick. Now go and bring the car round for Nora."

He obeyed her without a word.

Marion was filled with surprise at the decisiveness of Aunt Rosalie. It was so unexpected. Even Roderick seemed stunned by it.

Nora made a hasty breakfast then fled to collect the remainder of her things.

Rosalie stayed on in the diningroom, silent and thoughtful.

"Aunt," said Marion tentatively, and Rosalie looked up.

"Yes?"

"How did all that start? Nora and I only caught the end of it."

Rosalie sighed.

"It was Roderick, naturally. Tom said something about this girl he is engaged to, Bella. Roderick seized on it and egged him on to talk about her. It was as if he couldn't bear the idea of her being at Astonley, but he just had to know all there was to know about her, and the worse it was the more he had to probe."

"Is she really so very bad?"

"No, of course not. It's just that she *sounds* so unsuitable for this place. And I think Tom piled it on a bit at first, to tease Roderick. But it went beyond a joke quickly enough."

"But what is wrong with her?"

"She sounds like a horrid little gold digger, but I can't believe it. Tom seems a very decent sort. I don't think he would be taken in. But you never know with men," she ended doubtfully, "According to Tom, she worked in a beauty parlour, did manicures or something, married a rich old client and then divorced him after a few years. The divorce settlement is financing her trip to Europe, I gather."

"Oh." Marion was ashamed at the sudden boiling resentment of this unknown woman which engulfed her. It was unthinkable that Astonley should be hers.

"The trouble with us," said Rosalie suddenly, as if she had read Marion's mind, "is that we think too much of this place. We all hated the idea of Tom because he was a stranger, and we were afraid that he might drag Astonley down in some way. Now we are thinking the same thing about Bella. It will do us the world of good to go away from here."

Marion looked down at the cloth, tracing the pattern of the damask with one finger.

"I shall be glad to go, Aunt. It's all changed. Everyone has changed."

"That's growing up, Marion," said Rosalie softly, "It happens to all of us. When we are children we only see people from our own narrow angle. We don't see them as they really are. It's quite a shock when we do."

"But it has happened so quickly," Marion burst out, "Last week you seemed to turn into strangers, all of you."

"That was because of the circumstances. You weren't alone, Marion. We were all affected by it. Wondering if it could be possible that one of us is a murderer. It hit you hardest because you were so unprepared. Forgive me, so very young for your age, too. You have had to do your growing-up all in a matter of a few days. It's bound to hurt."

Marion flushed.

"I suppose you mean about James. I must have been very naïve."

"That wasn't really your fault. Some people never lose a certain childishness. My father-in-law was one of them. He would never believe that James was wild. He insisted that it was just boyish high spirits and that James would settle down. He wouldn't let any of it be mentioned in your hearing. Even when Alice appeared on the scene, he would have it that she had snared James into marrying her against his will."

"It wasn't true," said Marion jerkily.

Rosalie looked at her curiously.

"I don't imagine that it was. I'm glad you realise it. I was afraid that you were going to let James spoil your life."

Marion shook her head. She was only too afraid that James had succeeded in spoiling her life without any willingness on her part.

"You'll meet some nice boy and marry and raise a family of your own," Rosalie went on, "You wait till we get to London. We will have a much wider circle then."

The prospect failed to cheer Marion.

"You've wanted to live in London for ages, haven't you?" she asked, not to appear ungrateful.

For a moment, Rosalie did not answer.

"It's almost a family joke," she said at last, "My wanting to go back to London. Don't you remember how Robert used to goad me into complaining about country life, just to tease me. Now that I am going, I think I shall miss Astonley. Silly, isn't it?"

And with that she hurried out of the room.

Marion, left to herself, knew that she ought to go to her room to start packing her things, for the move over to the Dower House, and, later, the move to London. Instead, she went out into the garden. There she found Bertie Hough, the gardener, gazing down gloomily at her own patch. The little garden was bright with flowers and scented.

"Ah," he said, by way of greeting.

"It will be all yours now," Marion told him, "I shall be going to live in London soon."

Hough grunted.

"There's a wasps' nest in it," he complained, "I'll have to get some stuff for it on Monday."

He ambled away, leaving Marion torn between indignation and laughter. She might have known that he would express no pleasure in his little victory. But it was a bit much to blame her for having a wasps' nest in her patch.

"What's so funny?" he demanded a voice behind her.

It was Tom.

"I'm glad somebody can find a laugh this morning," he went on.

She went to him.

"Tom, I'm so sorry about all this. Truly."

He passed a hand over the back of his neck.

"To be honest, Marion, so am I. Roderick needed to be taught a lesson, but I overdid it. I lost my temper."

"You were sticking up for Bella. You were entitled to do that."

A brief smile touched his mouth.

"Loyal Marion! You're not angry with me?"

"No, of course not. You were quite justified in being angry with Roderick."

"I shouldn't have turned his mother out of the Dower House. What should I do, Marion? Apologise?"

Marion hesitated.

"It's not fair to shove it off on to your shoulders," Tom went on quickly.

Rosalie appeared round the side of the house. She stopped when she saw Tom.

It was too late to turn back. He had seen her and was walking towards her.

"Look, Rosalie," he said, "I lost my temper just now. I apologise."

"I think we should be the ones to do that, Tom," she replied.

Tom heaved a sigh of relief.

"Let's take it as said then. Shake?"

Even Rosalie had to smile at his obvious eagerness to make friends. She shook hands with him.

"And you can stay on in the Dower House for as long as you like," he said.

"No, Tom, it will be better if we go. Marion will tell you that I have wanted to go back to London for years. And Roderick won't change, you know. It will be better for all of us, and that includes your future wife, if we go. We will be away from here by the time that she arrives. Now, if you will excuse me, I'm very busy."

Quickly she retraced her steps and disappeared in the direction of the front door. A car horn tooted.

"That must be Nora, just going," said Marion, "I must say goodbye to her."

Tom grinned.

"I'd better not show my face. Roderick and I had best keep out of each other's way for a while. Give her my good wishes. And tell Rosalie I'm clearing out, straight away. It will be better if I do. See if you can get her to change her mind about going, won't you?"

"I'll try. I must fly, or Nora will be gone."

Tom's voice called her back as she reached the corner of the house.

"Marion!"

She paused.

"Yes?"

He gave her a twisted smile.

"I'll be sorry if you aren't here when I come back." The smile vanished suddenly. "Lord! what a mess all this is. Why the hell couldn't I have met you sooner?"

CHAPTER 13

At ten o'clock on Monday morning, Alec Liston, Director of Internal Security, walked into his Deputy's office.

"Charles," he said abruptly, "What have you been doing to Superintendent Beech?"

Charles Warren looked up from the pile of papers on his desk. In his opinion most of what lay before him was just a load of bumpf, but that was one of the penalties of being chairbound. In the old days it had been different. . . .

He was not sighing for the past. A lot of it was better not thought about. But first thing on Monday morning, he often experienced the urge to be up and out, scotching some dirty little traitor's game.

This Monday morning was one of those, but his dissatisfaction had roots far from the usual and nothing whatever to do with the Ministry of Security. And the last thing he wanted was a visit from his boss.

"Nothing much," he replied sourly, "Nothing at all compared with what I would *like* to do to him. What have you heard about it, anyway?"

He eyed Liston, a sleek, grey man, three years his senior, who rarely moved out of his office, but who yet managed to collect a surprising amount of information. Charles had known him for thirty-odd years, since prep school days, but Alec was still an enigma. Yet, in all probability, Charles was his nearest approach to a friend. It was a love-hate relationship. Latterly, Charles had found himself liking

Liston more than ever before. This morning could well set them back to the beginning, for Liston could not be expected to approve of Charles interfering with a police investigation.

"Oh, I have my little methods," said Liston airily, infuriatingly, "But I would like to hear your side of it."

"It was just a case of being on the spot, quite by chance. Beech seemed to think I had engineered it deliberately and came rushing at me like a bull at a gate," said Charles, and gave him an outline of the events at Winsmere.

"Such an exciting life you lead," Liston commented, "You can't even go visiting your wife's grandfather without running into a bunch of murderers. The point is, are you taking any further interest in the matter?"

Charles looked him straight in the eye.

"Do you really want to know?"

There was a pause, while Liston stared back at him. Clearly he had also heard about Inspector Morton's visit on Friday afternoon, and had put two and two together. Charles was certain that Alec could make an accurate guess at what the Inspector had wanted.

"Morton is a very able man," said Liston musingly, confirming Charles's suspicions. "It is a difficult situation for him. Yes, on the whole, I would like to know if you are going on with this. I am aware that you will do as you please, Charles, and since I don't want to lose your valuable services, you can take it that I should pretend tactfully that I did not know what you were up to, if I did not think that I might lend a hand, too."

Here was a surprise.

"Alec, what are you getting at?" demanded Charles suspiciously.

Liston raised a hand deprecatingly.

"Dear boy, I assure you I have no ulterior motives. Merely a schoolboy desire to get my own back on Superintendent Beech. You weren't the only one to find him tiresome."

It would be an immense advantage to have Liston's backing.

"All Morton has asked me to do is have a go at the post office clerk. It would be a help if he remembered if the telegram was handed in by a man or a woman."

"Let's go ahead on him, then. I'm sure he will split himself, flogging his memory, once he knows that we are interested. Most officials," Liston added complacently, "are scared stiff of us."

Charles laughed, pushed aside his papers, and made his way to the busy post office from which the fatal telegram had been sent.

He was wasting his time. A flustered postmaster, eyeing Charles's credentials nervously, explained that the clerk in question, Ben Price, had been working out his notice at the time that the telegram was handed in. That was on the Thursday. He was interviewed by the police on the Friday. And on the Saturday he left. Charles smothered his irritation and asked for the man's address.

There, too, he drew a blank. Ben Price had quit his digs on Monday morning, without leaving a forwarding address.

Charles went back to the post office. There he discovered that Price had been a quiet little man, and no one knew very much about him. He had worked there for three months. Now he was gone. And that was that. One of the women had a vague idea that he might have come from the West Country; she half-recalled that he had spoken of it once; though it might have been Wales, she thought belatedly; he did have a slight accent.

Thoroughly irritated, Charles returned to his own office.

"It's hardly worth bothering about," he complained to

Liston, "but I did promise Morton. I'll send out a routine circular. I've a description of sorts. About five feet seven, brown hair, grey eyes, no distinguishing marks. Age : middle forties. How many million do you suppose that could apply to? And even if we did find him, it's highly doubtful if he could be of any help at all. However," he concluded with a frustrated sigh, "it's worth a try."

"What about the people who gave references for him when he applied for the post office job?" suggested Liston. "There must have been at least a couple."

"I have their addresses. But if he's a wanderer, and it looks as though he is, they may not know where he is now."

He had to tell Morton. Reluctantly he picked up the telephone. As he dialled the code number, he thought it was a pity that he had proved a broken reed so quickly. Morton was a good policeman. It must have been a severe blow to his pride to have to ask for help from outside the Force.

Much good it had done him.

The Inspector listened quietly while Charles broke the bad news.

"I doubt if he would have been any good to us," he commented resignedly, "Thanks anyway, Mr Warren."

"Is there anything else I can do?"

"I don't think there is, thanks," Morton sounded tired, "The Superintendent is visiting Shropshire tomorrow. I have an idea that he might make an arrest."

"Marion?"

"Who else?"

The atmosphere of the Dower House was anything but happy. It was a comfortable late eighteenth century house, erected by the first Winter to live at Astonley. He was a wealthy banker, the founder of the family fortunes, who had bought the place from the impoverished branch of the

Kenyons who had held the manor for centuries. He had built the house for his widowed mother. Succeeding generations of widows had lived in it. Rosalie had been there for nearly twenty years.

Now she was busy packing for the move to London, scrupulously listing all the items of furniture which belonged to Astonley and therefore must remain in the house: deciding which pieces would have to go into store; sorting through the accumulation of years. And all of it with a set face and grim determination.

Marion, set to helping Roderick clear the attic, thought the place was little better than a prison. Mother and son scarcely exchanged a word, and when they did the merest remark could spark off a quarrel.

It was hot up there under the roof, and the tiny windows had not been opened in living memory. Roderick struggled in vain to persuade one to admit a breath of air. And the attic was full of junk.

From downstairs came the mellow tones of an old clock announcing that it was noon. Roderick stood up, covered with dust and so unlike his usual self that Marion giggled.

He glowered at her.

"Come on. Let's pack it in."

She sat back on her heels. She, too, had had enough.

"There's a lot left to do," she said disconsolately.

"We ought to cart it all downstairs and burn it."

"We can't do that. Some of the stuff here is quite good. It's only a matter of sorting it out. There'll be a big enough bonfire for you at the end just from the rubbish."

"It's all rubbish as far as I am concerned," Roderick replied, "Are you coming down, or are you not?"

Marion scrambled to her feet.

"I'm coming."

Rosalie met them on the first floor landing, frowning.

"Have you finished?"

"No," said Roderick grimly, "But I'm not doing any more today. Marion can if she wants. I'm going out this afternoon. I've had enough."

Unexpectedly, Rosalie's frown vanished.

"So have I," she admitted, "It was a mistake to work all over the weekend, though I thought it would be better to get on with the horrible job. And I have driven you two poor things mercilessly. I think we all should take the afternoon off."

No one suggested that the three of them should go out together. They had all been too much in each other's company for the past forty-eight hours. And it seemed that they could not leave the house fast enough. They made a hasty lunch, then Roderick was away down the drive in his little sports car before two o'clock. Within twenty minutes Rosalie drove off, more sedately, in her saloon. Marion walked over to Astonley to collect the little runabout which Uncle Robert had given her for her twenty-first birthday.

She drove down into Winsmere, through the village, and out on to the Oldchurch road. She was in sight of the first houses of the town when, suddenly, she changed her mind and swung sharply left. The lane led her with many twists and turns to an open space of heathland, once fenced and gated, but now the barriers had disintegrated and the place was open to all comers. Long ago it had been an airfield; the old concrete road round the perimeter was still there, and dotted here and there air-raid shelters and the skeletons of abandoned huts could be seen. A quiet, deserted place, where a few sheep, unattended, grazed on the disused runways. A favourite spot for the courting couples of the district.

Today it suited Marion's mood. She parked the car, found herself a sunny slope on the side of an old shelter, and stretched out on the grass. . . .

A drop of cold water splashed on to her face.

Marion blinked and sat up. A chilly puff of wind set her shivering, while more drops of water fell on her hands and bare legs.

She had slept, warmed by the afternoon sun. Now clouds covered the sky and the sudden cold had roused her.

She looked at her watch. Four o'clock.

There was a crash of thunder and the storm broke on her, sending her running for the shelter of the car.

She decided that she might as well go home. It was too wet to stay on the airfield, and she had no desire to go into Oldchurch. She would be sure to meet someone she knew—and who would surely want to talk about the murders.

The very thought made her shiver again. In spite of herself, she wondered how the police investigation was progressing. It was unthinkable that the crimes should be written off as unsolved. It was equally unthinkable that any of the family could be involved.

She was so absorbed in her thoughts that she missed her usual turning. She reached a crossroads, and realised her mistake. It was not worth turning back. The road ahead would take her to Winsmere by a devious route. She was in no hurry.

A mile further up the road she saw a couple of cars parked at the edge of a wood. With a little shock of surprise she recognised both of them.

One was Aunt Rosalie's and the other belonged to Dr Ludlow.

Automatically, Marion slowed down to crawl past them. Both cars were empty.

She picked up speed again. It was nothing to do with her, and there was bound to be some easy explanation. Dr Ludlow must have been visiting a patient, and Aunt Rosalie—

Whatever could Aunt Rosalie be doing there?

And there was no house, or cottage, or even a caravan in sight which might contain a patient for the doctor.

And where were they? The only possible answer was in the wood.

Sheltering from the rain?

It was all very odd. If it had been any two other people, Marion would have suspected a secret meeting. But Aunt Rosalie and Geoffrey Ludlow? The thing didn't make sense. They could meet in Winsmere any day of the week.

Marion was the first home. The others did not return until after six o'clock. And no one offered an account of how they had spent the afternoon.

Conversation dwindled in an atmosphere of gloom. Marion found herself watching the other two. Aunt Rosalie was so wrapped in thought that every remark addressed to her had to be repeated, while Roderick sulked.

"I think you had better go to London, Roderick," Rosalie said briskly, suddenly pulling herself together at nine o'clock in the evening. "We must have some sort of accommodation. You go and have a look round, and if you can find two or three places for me to look at, I can run up to Town and glance over them. I have too much to do here to be away for long."

"I've been thinking," he replied, "Couldn't we move into James's place for a week or two, while we are looking round? It's not bad, though I don't care for Alice's taste in decoration."

Marion looked up.

"I didn't know you had been there," she blurted.

"I really don't think I could go to that house," Rosalie stared at her son, appalled, "Just think what happened there."

Roderick laughed.

"That was nothing to do with the house. And they both died in hospital, if you feel squeamish about that. I can't see why you should. Some pretty sordid things may well have happened in this house, let alone what horrors they are certain to have got up to at Astonley over the years."

"No," said Rosalie stubbornly, "I will not go there. And another thing, it belongs to Tom now."

"I'm sure he would be only too pleased to let you have it if you wanted it," Marion put in.

Rosalie gave her a sharp look.

"I've no doubt that he would."

Marion felt her colour rising. She had not meant to speak out of turn. She had only thought that it might ease the situation, and she knew that Tom would seize any chance to re-establish good relations with Rosalie. But the bitter truth was that it was not for her to say so.

"I wouldn't think of asking him," Rosalie was saying, "We are on our own now. And I certainly don't want to offer to buy it from him." There was the sound of a car on the gravel of the drive outside the house. Rosalie crossed to the window and peered out. "Good heavens! It's Inspector Morton. What can he be wanting now?"

She hurried out into the hall.

A moment later they heard her exclaim loudly. Roderick leapt to his feet and dashed out into the hall, Marion at his heels.

"Mother! What has happened?"

Rosalie was leaning against the wall, her hands over her face.

"I'll tell them," said Inspector Morton grimly, his sharp eyes watching both young people closely. "A dead body has been found on the old airfield. A woman, whom we have reason to believe was on her way here."

"Here?" echoed Roderick sharply, "We weren't expecting anyone. Who was she?"

"An American by the name of Arabella Manston."

"Tom's fiancée," gasped Marion.

"So Mrs Winter tells me," agreed Morton.

"But what was she doing there? How did she die?"

"She was strangled with a piece of thin wire, Miss Loring. You know what that means. Murder."

CHAPTER 14

"RIGHT, Inspector, let's see what you've got for me," said Superintendent Beech, rubbing his hands in anticipation, "Filthy morning, isn't it? Weather's properly broken, at last. Can't do with all that heat, myself."

Morton laid an already bulky folder in front of his superior, who had just arrived in Oldchurch from London.

"It's all there, sir. Fortunately, the rain held off while we were searching the airfield. There was just the one thunderstorm around four o'clock, then it was dry until the early hours." He glanced out of the window. "Looks as though it is set in now."

He was obtaining an obscure satisfaction from the thought that Beech would be wishing the hot weather back again when he was tramping over the soaking airfield.

Beech was leafing through the file.

"I'll read all this later," he said. "You tell me."

"The body was found shortly after seven o'clock, by a courting couple. It was lying behind an old air-raid shelter, but it wasn't actually hidden. It was bound to be found fairly quickly. There were a couple of suitcases lying near the body and her handbag was found a short distance away. In it we found that letter."

"Ah, yes," said Beech, searching in the folder. He extracted a single sheet of writing paper, with the envelope pinned to it. "Dearest Bella," he read, "The situation here has changed, and I want you to come to Astonley at once. Never mind about Scotland. We can go there together later. Come on Monday. There is a train leaving London at one, which arrives in Oldchurch at four. I'll meet you at the station. Don't fail me. It's vital that you come. If you don't, I shall know that you don't really care for me. But I know you will. Sorry I have had to type this letter, but I have hurt my hand and find it difficult to hold a pen. With all my love." He looked up. "Signed T."

"Thomas Winter. Or so we are supposed to believe. Certainly that poor woman did. But for one thing, he hasn't hurt his hand. And for another, he left for a Continental holiday on Saturday morning."

Beech nodded.

"We shall get him back soon enough," he said, "I've sent an inquiry to all the Channel ports, and to the police over the other side. Not that we really need him to tell us that he didn't write that letter. The point is, who did? How far have you got with it?"

"No prints, of course. Just smudges. Nothing we can use. But it came from Astonley itself. It was typed on the machine in the study there. It was posted on Saturday morning. The postmark says Oldchurch, but that doesn't mean to say that it was posted here. The mail from all the surrounding districts, including Winsmere, goes through this office. The post is collected in the village at midday. Any of them could have posted it. Or typed it, for that matter. There was a lot of coming and going at Astonley that morning."

"Oh, why particularly?"

"There had been a family row, sir, and Mrs Winter and Roderick had been given their marching orders. So they were transferring their things back to the Dower House. And they were taking Miss Loring with them. On top of that, the nurse was leaving, and somebody had to take her into Oldchurch to catch the train. That was Roderick Winter. The family," Morton added, "aren't very forthcoming on the subject of that row, though they can't deny it, and they have spent the weekend sorting out the stuff at the Dower House ready for moving out in a couple of weeks. All this on top of Thomas Winter's announcement that he is engaged to be married, and his taking off unexpectedly on a holiday. It isn't very difficult to add that one up. The whole village has got it that the family didn't react properly to the engagement, and that sent the balloon up."

"Could be," agreed Beech, "We will go into that later. They needn't think that they can hold out on me. To get back to this letter. I can fill you in on the London end. It arrived at the hotel on Monday morning. Mrs Manston had palled up with one of the other guests. They shared a table in the diningroom, so she was there when Mrs Manston opened the letter, at breakfast-time. Mrs Manston was supposed to be leaving for Scotland later that day. But naturally that letter made her change her mind. She left at lunchtime, presumably to catch the train suggested in the letter."

"She was in Oldchurch at four o'clock," Morton told him, "The storm broke just as she was passing through the barrier at the station. The ticket collector remembers an American woman making some comment on the English weather. It must have been Mrs Manston, though the man's description is a bit vague."

"Did he see anybody meet her?"

Morton shook his head.

"Not for sure. He says he saw her standing sheltering for a moment, and there was a fair girl beside her, but whether she was meeting Mrs Manston or was just another passenger he couldn't say. However it was, they weren't there for any length of time. He didn't see them go, either singly or together."

"A fair girl. You know what I am thinking, Inspector. Well, go on."

"It takes about a quarter of an hour to drive to the old airfield. It was raining hard, and no one saw a car around there. But we know that there must have been. Two, in fact."

"Oh?"

"That was the first rain we've had for weeks, sir. But there are two sets of tyre tracks in a patch of mud near the air-raid shelter where the body was found. They must have been made that day. After four o'clock."

"And have you found the cars which made those tracks?" inquired Beech softly.

"One of them, sir." Morton was surprised at his own reluctance in giving the information. "It belongs to Miss Marion Loring. She admits that she was at the airfield yesterday afternoon. She says she left there when the rain began, and came straight home. Unfortunately, we have only her word for it."

"She will have to do better than that," said Beech, and laughed.

"In fairness to her," Morton said stolidly, "It doesn't look as though she typed that letter. I've had it tested thoroughly. It was typed by someone using only a few fingers, not by an experienced typist. Which she is."

The satisfied expression did not leave Beech's face.

"Don't let that put you off, Inspector. People know a damn sight too much about police methods nowadays. They know we can tell the difference between touch typing and the two-fingered stuff. So remember this: if you can't type properly, that's all there is to it; but there is nothing to stop an experienced typist behaving like an amateur and using only a couple of fingers."

Rosalie was sorting through the linen cupboard with an air of grim determination.

"There! That pile of towels can be packed. Take them into the spare room, will you, Marion?"

Obediently, Marion picked up the towels.

"Oh, Mother," groaned Roderick from behind her, "can't you give this a rest?"

"It has to be done. We have little enough time."

"But the police have been charging round the place all morning."

Rosalie looked up from her task.

"I can't see what difference that makes, except to hinder us. Quite the reverse. It is just as well that we have something to do."

"But what were they *doing*?" Marion heard the tremor in her voice, and acknowledged that she was afraid. "They were using the typewriter in the study. I heard them. And they were looking round the cars. What did they want?"

"They don't tell us anything," complained Rosalie fretfully, "Not that I really want to know, but surely they can't suspect *us* of killing Bella?"

Roderick let out a hollow laugh.

"You can bet your boots that's just what they do think."

"But why? Why should any of us want to kill a perfect stranger?"

"To stop her marrying Thomas."

Rosalie gave up her assault on the linen. She turned round to stare at her son.

"Why, for heaven's sake?"

Roderick shrugged.

"Don't ask me. I don't know how their tiny minds work. But, depend upon it, Mother, it's us that they are after at the moment. Inspector Morton has only been holding his fire because he is waiting for Superintendent Beech to come back. We can expect *him* sometime today for sure."

Marion shuddered. The prospect of another interview with Beech filled her with dread.

"The thing is," Roderick continued, "How good are our alibis for yesterday afternoon? Can you account for every minute of your time, Mother?"

Rosalie returned to her work inside the cupboard.

"I was shopping in Oldchurch all afternoon," she said, "I don't suppose I can account for every minute. Who could? But I was in and out of shops, and I ended up having a cup of tea in a café. I met several people I knew."

Her voice rang with confidence, and for a moment Marion doubted what she had seen with her own eyes. Perhaps she had mistaken the car parked in the lane near the airfield. Then she glanced at Roderick. His face wore a satisfied smirk.

Rosalie was delving in the back of the cupboard.

"There are some old towels here," she said, and her voice sounded muffled. "They are too good to throw out." She backed away, her hands full of linen. She straightened up and faced the others, her cheeks flushed. "I wonder if David could use them up? Pop over with them, Marion, will you?"

It was a summary dismissal, so that she could be alone with her son.

Marion was glad enough to go, even though she had avoided David since his extraordinary proposal of marriage. She wasn't sure how she should greet him, whether she could manage to go on behaving as though it had never happened. She felt her colour rising as she entered his office.

David was a better dissembler than she. He was so exactly as he always was that Marion wondered if she could have dreamed the whole thing. But she knew that she had not. It struck her that whatever his motive in asking her to marry him, it had not been out of love. Only out of the most tepid affection. His indifference today rang too true to be assumed. It brought a chill into her heart.

But somehow she found herself telling him her fears.

"I can't face that man Beech again," she confessed, with the tears running unchecked down her face, "I would run away—if I could think of anywhere to run to!"

Gravely David handed her a large handkerchief. Marion mopped her streaming eyes with it.

"Would that be wise?"

Marion could not answer. She shook her head miserably.

"On the other hand," David went on quietly, "it might give us a bit more time. To find the real criminal, I mean. The problem is, where could you go?"

Marion stared up at him with new hope. Even to her own ears the suggestion of running away had sounded like madness. But if David thought it might work. . . .

"We could hire a private detective," he was saying, thinking aloud, "But where could we hide you in the meantime? My sister would help, I'm sure. They would never think of looking for you in Bristol, especially if I dropped them a hint that you were in London."

His words had given her an idea. She sprang up, hope filling her heart.

"I know!" she exclaimed, "David, it might work."

"I'll drive you part of the way," he offered eagerly, "And I'll phone Mary."

Marion shook her head.

"No, I don't want to go to your sister, thanks all the same. But I'll have to get away from here. I daren't show my face in Oldchurch. Could you drive me to Crewe? I can pick up a train there."

The eagerness had died out of his face.

"Yes, of course," he said quietly, "You'll need money. You can't stop off in Oldchurch to go to the bank. How are you fixed?"

Marion frowned.

"I hadn't thought of that. Oh, well, never mind, I'll manage."

David pulled out his wallet.

"You can take all I've got with me. It will be enough to keep you going for a little while. Marion, where will you go?"

But Marion shook her head.

"It will be better if no one knows."

If David felt snubbed, his face did not show it. Methodically, he counted out the notes which he extracted from his wallet.

"Twenty pounds. Will that do?"

"Amply. David, I really am very grateful." She reached to pick up the money, stumbled over the edge of a mat, and sent notes and all flying.

"Oh, how clumsy!" she apologised, on her knees gathering up the money and the contents of the wallet.

David laughed.

"No damage done." He bent to retrieve some of the cards and papers which had stuffed the wallet.

"That's everything I think," said Marion, scrambling to her feet and handing him a bundle of odds and ends. Her eye caught on a photograph, its edges much worn from a long sojourn in the wallet. With a shock, Marion recognised it.

It was of Flora Ludlow, the doctor's late wife.

Marion handed it to David, hoping that he had not noticed her interest. It was no business of hers, but it was strange that he should carry such a photograph. She eyed him covertly and wondered if she knew anything about him at all.

Inspector Morton was sitting inside a police car listening to a message over the radio. A few yards away from him, in the pouring rain, Superintendent Beech was peering under a tarpaulin which was protecting the telltale tyre tracks.

Morton sighed. The message was finished and he would have to go out into the wet again.

Then Beech came stamping back to the car.

"You've got casts of those, I suppose," he said, getting in, "What was the message?"

"Word from Dover, sir. Thomas Winter crossed over to France on Saturday night, taking his car with him. He hadn't a booking on the ferry, so he had to wait a fair time. Kicked up a bit of a fuss about it. There's no word from France yet about picking him up."

"Early yet," grunted Beech, "Let's get out and see that girl."

But Marion had fled from Astonley.

"There you are," Beech raged, "Proof. Innocent people don't bolt. She can't have got far. Send out a call for her. And make out a warrant for her arrest."

CHAPTER 15

Charles Warren gazed dubiously at his stacked in-tray. Momentarily he regretted his present advancement and wished that he were back as one of the rank and file. There were advantages, of course. In the old days he would not have had the settled homelife he now enjoyed. But the price was a load of paperwork.

He glanced at his watch. He had a meeting at ten. There was nothing for it: he would have to tackle the pile of papers.

The top one caught his interest immediately. It was a note from the man whom he had sent to check on the post office clerk's referees. The note was short and to the point.

It read:

"Both accommodation addresses. No further trace."

He stared at it for several minutes, ticking off possible meanings in his mind. Then he put it to one side. So Ben Price had written his own references. Alec Liston would be interested in that. Not to mention Inspector Morton.

The rest of the stuff was, to him, routine. He worked through it steadily, keeping an eye on the time and steadfastly refusing to let his imagination wander off into idle speculations about murder. He had just picked up the last item in the in-tray when Alec Liston walked into the office.

"It's that meeting in five minutes, Charles. Are you ready?"

"I think so. Why do we both have to go?"

Liston shrugged.

"You know the Home Office. Fussy. What's that you have there?"

Charles handed him a photograph, to which was attached a sheet of paper.

"Routine inquiry from Interpol. The French police have a corpse they can't identify. That can't be anything new."

Liston read through the scanty information.

"Male. About thirty. Medium height. Brown hair. Clean-shaven. Scar on abdomen. Found in a ditch outside Boulogne at 4 p.m. yesterday. Dead about three hours. Garrotted with thin wire. Clothing: underwear, British and worn; trousers, shirt and jacket American, newish. Anyone we are interested in?"

Charles shrugged.

"Not to my knowledge. I'll circulate it. O.K., I'm ready now." The telephone rang. Charles picked it up. "Yes? . . . *Who*?" He covered the phone with his hand. "Alec, Marion Loring is downstairs asking for me."

Liston's eyebrows shot up.

"Well! Your fatal charm. There's a warrant out for her arrest."

"Is there?"

"I had come in to tell you that, when you diverted me with that French corpse."

Charles spoke into the telephone.

"Send her up, please. To my secretary's office." He replaced the receiver. "I'll talk to her after that meeting."

"*We* will, you mean," Liston corrected him.

"You want to be in on this?"

"But of course," Liston rejoined lightly, "I like to know what you are up to."

Charles followed him down the corridor, reflecting that, while he liked Alec Liston a lot better these days than in the past, there were still times when it was difficult to be sure that his little "jokes" were not deadly serious.

In the meantime, Marion was safe. Not that he could give her sanctuary for any length of time. But it would be interesting to know how it was that she had left Astonley with Beech in hot pursuit.

The meeting was as tedious as he had feared. And long-drawn-out. It was past midday before Charles and Liston returned to the Ministry of Security.

"Now for Marion," said Charles with satisfaction and rang for his secretary.

"Miss Loring is waiting in my office," the woman told him, "Shall I bring her in? Oh, and there has been a call for you from the C.I.D. in Bristol. In response to your inquiry about a Benjamin Price. They are sending you the information and a photograph."

Charles and Liston exchanged glances.

"It doesn't sound much like our man," said Charles doubtfully. "Not if he is known to the police. The post office people were all quite definite that he was a quiet and sober citizen."

"Lying low," suggested Liston.

"Could be. Ah, here is Marion."

The girl was pale and there were dark circles under her eyes. She glanced fearfully at Liston who had taken up an observer's position at the side of Charles's desk.

"I may be a complete fool," she burst out, "but I had to get away from Astonley. I couldn't face Superintendent Beech again. So I came here. It was the only place I could think of. If you can't help me, nobody can."

"I'm afraid that Superintendent Beech must be hopping mad with you," Charles said quietly, "When did you leave?"

"Yesterday afternoon. David drove me over to Crewe. I picked up a train there. I suppose they are looking for me?"

"They are. Where did you spend the night?"

"In a little hotel near Euston. It was rather horrid, but I couldn't have faced any of my friends. I was too late arriving to contact you last night."

"I think I ought to tell you right away that there is a warrant out for your arrest."

Marion gasped.

"Also, I can't keep you here indefinitely," he went on, "I shall have to surrender you to the police."

Marion clasped her hands together and looked at the floor.

"I see."

"But not just—yet," Liston put in.

The girl stared up at him.

"I don't understand."

"He means that we have a few hours' grace," Charles explained, smiling at her, "If we are to help you we need a lot of information from you. Now is our chance to obtain it. Once we have handed you over to Superintendent Beech we may not be able to get at you for a while."

Marion shuddered, but retained control.

"But I don't know anything," she protested.

Liston laughed.

"You will be surprised what you find that you know. Don't look so scared. We don't use truth drugs on people. Nor instruments of torture. Remember we are on your side."

"Why should you be?" asked Marion straightly.

"Just be glad that we are," Liston recommended. He turned to Charles. "I think it would be better if we used one of the interrogation rooms."

Marion was sent off under the escort of the secretary.

Charles gathered up notebook and pencil and prepared to follow.

"Alec," he said suddenly, "You could give me a couple of days' leave or something."

"What for?"

"To have a go at this thing. After all, it's not our job. There could be repercussions if it got about."

"We shall be saving the taxpayers' money if we prove that girl is innocent before it comes to the matter of a trial. Besides, I rather fancy myself as a detective nowadays."

Inspector Morton looked glumly at his superior.

"Have we got enough to hold her?"

"Maybe not," Beech admitted, "but if the ticket collector at the station here can pick her out of a line-up as the one who was with the Manston woman, and if that rag-and-bone man can do the same so that we can prove she was in the vicinity of James Winter's house on the second of June, then we've got her."

"If," murmured Morton, although he knew it was asking for trouble.

Anger flamed in Beech's eyes for a moment.

"Still not convinced?"

"No, sir."

"Then who is your candidate for a long spell at the taxpayers' expense?"

"Same as before, sir, Roderick Winter. Lots of folks would think that a place like Astonley would be worth killing for, if you could get away with it. It's probably been done before, and successfully, too."

"No police forces then," commented Beech, "But kindly explain to me, Inspector, just *how* young Roderick pulled it off?"

Morton shook his head.

"I can't," he admitted, "But it galls me to see him getting away with it."

"You want to forget that," Beech advised him, "You've

let that young twerp get your goat. It's the girl, all right. She has run away, hasn't she?"

"We don't know where she has gone," Morton pointed out, "Nor why."

Beech's clenched fist crashed down on the desk.

"It beats me how the hell an inexperienced chit like her could drop out of sight for twenty-four minutes, let alone twenty-four hours. No news?"

Inactivity invariably raised Beech to boiling point. Morton was thankful to see him stamp off to his hotel for his tea. He was even more thankful that the Superintendent was off the premises when a call from London came through just before five o'clock. He hastened to phone an edited version of it to his superior.

"The girl has turned up, sir. She fetched up at the Ministry of Security. Mr Warren is bringing her back to Astonley tonight."

At the other end of the line, Beech was breathing heavily through his nose. It was too much to hope, thought Morton, that the news would bring on a fit of apoplexy.

Marion lay back against the deep upholstery of the big car, and watched the countryside flying by. She had never felt more tired in her life. Tired and drained.

Literally, she thought ruefully. Drained of every scrap of information about Astonley, the Winters, their neighbours, herself. The afternoon at the Ministry had turned into a nightmare, under the ruthless and persistent questioning and cross-questioning. Yet this had been done in a spirit of kindness. She shuddered to think how these terrible men would treat an enemy.

Superintendent Beech could do his worst. His technique was infantile compared with that of these frightening allies she had acquired.

But they were allies. They had worn down her every

defence, drawn out the most closely guarded secrets. Now they must know her better than she knew herself. And at the end they had both told her that they believed her.

She could face the Superintendent now.

They went straight to the Dower House. Charles pulled up alongside a police car, parked by the front door. From the front passenger seat, Hope Warren turned to Marion, in the back.

"It looks as though they are waiting for us. Are you all right?"

Marion summoned up a smile. She was glad that Hope had insisted on coming too. Here, at least, was someone whom she had known, on and off, for most of her life, and who was exactly what she seemed. Marion trusted Charles implicitly, but she was more than a little afraid of him now.

Their arrival had been heard. The front door was open, and there were people spilling out on to the steps. Beech and Inspector Morton and a couple of constables, one of them a woman. Behind them were Aunt Rosalie and Roderick and David. Marion found that her knees were shaking as she left the car.

Then suddenly another car swept up to the house and out of it jumped Tom.

He gazed round at them wildly.

"You've killed her. Bella. My Bella. Come on now, which one of you was it?"

CHAPTER 16

CHARLES and Hope stayed overnight in Winsmere, accepting the eager hospitality of her grandfather.

"Terrible business, this," muttered Sir John, "I can't think why anyone should want to murder that unfortunate young woman. And it is beyond me why the police should think that any of the people at Astonley could have done it. They had never even seen her, I understand. It must have been someone who followed her from London."

"I don't see how it can have been. There is that letter which lured her here," Charles pointed out.

Sir John was not convinced.

"And on the old airfield, too," he went on, as if that made it all the worse, "I know it well. Used to go rabbitting up there years ago. It was a bit of heath before they made it into a landing ground during the war. Why, only last Easter, I was recommending the place to a scout master we had round here looking for a camping site for his boys. I hope he decided against it. Their parents wouldn't care for it at all now."

Morning brought visitors. The first one, demanding Charles, arrived before breakfast was finished.

"I'm David Kenyon-Winter," he introduced himself, "I saw you last night, but in all that uproar I didn't manage to get a word with you."

Charles looked at him curiously. This man was still much of an unknown quantity. That had emerged clearly from Marion's interrogation. Until recently she had accepted him as part of the surroundings, the way children do with adults among whom they grow up. But not now.

"I was only trying to help Marion," David was saying, "That's why I agreed to drive her to Crewe. I see now that it has made things so much worse for her."

"Running away does give a bad impression," Charles agreed, studying him. David's position was unique. A well-paid employee, acting in his professional capacity, yet at the same time a connection of the family. It would be interesting to know his true opinion of the whole thing.

But David was non-committal. Astutely, he turned aside Charles's probing questions. It was difficult to decide if it was intentional evasion or an overwhelming absorption in Marion's fate.

"What will happen to her?" he demanded over again.

Charles shrugged.

"It's not for me to say."

"But you must have some sort of official standing," David persisted.

"No."

"But Marion ran to you." David's face darkened. He stood up abruptly. "I'm sorry. I'm wasting your time."

He left with the curtest of farewells.

"What's the matter with David?" asked Hope wonderingly, as she joined her husband in the hall, "He came past me just now with a face like thunder. He didn't even see me."

"I'm afraid he has misconstrued Marion's flight. I think that was jealousy, pure and simple," his eyes narrowed, "Unless that was the impression he intended to give."

"Who? David?" demanded Sir John, coming up behind them, "What's going on?"

"Is David interested in Marion?" asked Hope.

Sir John shook his head.

"Most unlikely I should think. I've never seen any sign of it."

"But he has never married. I'm sure it can't be for lack of chances. He is very presentable."

"He's a very self-contained sort of fellow, David. Doesn't wear his heart on his sleeve. But if you ask me, he's proud. His family has come down in the world and I reckon he feels it. He keeps himself to himself. Robert Winter used to have a devil of a job to persuade him to visit Astonley on a social basis. David takes after the Kenyons. He's the model of his maternal grandfather, the last earl. And where are the Kenyons now? All daughters, so the title's gone. Money gone. House gone. Must be pretty galling. One branch of the family built Astonley, but it was small beer to them compared with the rest of the property. Not that David has ever complained. And he is damned good at his job. Robert told me many a time that he considered himself lucky to have him."

All of which, thought Charles gloomily, takes me no nearer to understanding David Kenyon-Winter. And the most inexplicable thing of all was why he had put it into Marion's head to run away. For Charles was sure that he had. Marion herself was convinced that it was her own idea, but Charles knew well enough that, had it not been for David's backing, it would have remained a pipe dream.

The next visitor was Inspector Morton, half-way through the morning.

"I hoped you might still be here, Mr Warren. When are you due back in London?"

"I shall have to be in the office tomorrow morning. What's the situation here?"

Morton sighed.

"Superintendent Beech is on his way back to London. With Miss Loring."

"Under arrest?"

"Not exactly. Just helping. You know. He wants that rag and bone man to have a look at her."

"What about this end, the ticket collector at the station?"

Morton grinned.

"Proper funny that was, Mr Warren. He didn't pick her out of the line. I reckon he's one of those who doesn't like to commit himself. Beech was wild."

"I can imagine," Charles commented dryly, "What happens now?"

"I carry on, on my own lines. I don't know what Beech will do. If the rag and bone man doesn't turn up trumps, he will have to let Miss Loring go."

"So you still fancy Roderick?"

"I do. Though I'll admit I can't see where this latest murder fits in."

"Could he have done it?"

"Maybe. His story is that he went into Oldchurch to a couple of shops, then drove off into the country to get a bit of fresh air and be out of the atmosphere at Astonley for a while. Not much of an alibi, but it has the advantage that it is virtually unprovable, in either direction. And one thing is certain; his car wasn't one of those which left tracks on the airfield on Monday afternoon. Not that that means a thing. The old perimeter track is concrete, and, although it is broken in places, if he stuck to it he would be reasonably safe. We're having an appeal put out on the radio for anyone who was up at the airfield on Monday to come forward. If we could eliminate the other car it would be a help. You never know, we might find a witness who saw another car up there."

"And Roderick could have typed the letter which brought the Manston woman here in the first place. Easy enough to meet her at the station and say that Tom couldn't come and had sent him in his place. She wouldn't have suspected a thing. The point is: why should Roderick need to kill her at all?"

"It has to be the same motive throughout," Morton replied, "If he killed the others for the estate, then she had to go for the same reason."

"I can't see how it would benefit him. It isn't as though she was already married to Tom and was producing an heir."

"As far as we know."

Charles stared for a moment, then laughed.

"It's possible. It strikes me that we don't know nearly enough about Arabella Manston."

Inspector Morton smiled.

"There's a woman at the hotel in Cromwell Road who was quite friendly with her," he hinted.

There was perfect understanding between them. Once again Charles wished that all policemen were of Morton's stamp.

"I'll tackle her first thing in the morning," he promised.

The late train pulled into Oldchurch station. Some dozen passengers alighted and began making their way along the deserted platforms. Marion was the last to leave the train, stepping down uncertainly into the warm night.

She was tired and there was so much that she did not understand, but for the moment she was free again. She had stood in that humiliating line-up for the second time that day, and the old man had wandered up and down in front of them, peering at each one in turn. In the end he had gone away and she had been led off into a waiting room. She was there for a long time, then there was a further interview with Superintendent Beech. After that she was driven to the station and put on the train, sternly admonished to go back to Astonley and stay there. No more running off. The Superintendent would be in touch with her again.

She wondered if there would be anyone to meet her. No one had mentioned if a message had been passed to Astonley, and in her stupor she had not thought to ask. It was late, but there might be the odd taxi hanging around. She quickened her pace.

A voice said, "Marion!"

She stopped, stared about her. There, under a lamp, stood Tom.

"Come on," he said cheerfully, tucking her hand under his arm, "You must be fagged out. Come home."

She stumbled along beside him.

"Inspector Morton rang through," Tom was explaining, "Luckily, I took the call. I'm glad I could be the one to meet you."

He managed everything: handed her ticket to the collector, settled her in the waiting car, made sure she was comfortable.

"Tom, you're so kind," she said as they rolled down the station drive.

"It's about time someone was kind to you, Marion."

"Then you don't believe I'm guilty?"

He let out a crack of laughter.

"The idea would be funny if it weren't so damn serious, with that clunk of a copper breathing down your neck. But at least he has had the sense to let you go now."

"Reluctantly," Marion admitted. Already she felt ten times better and she was grateful. "Tom, I haven't had a chance to say how sorry I am. About Bella, I mean."

He sighed and drove on in silence for a while.

"I wanted to explain to you, about Bella," he said suddenly.

"Explain to me? But why should you?"

"You know perfectly well what I mean, Marion. I'm not

the sort of fellow to play around with women. I'm twenty-eight and until recently I never even thought of getting married. I didn't get a very good impression of married life from my folks. They didn't get on together and I reckon it was a real relief to Ma when Dad died. Then I inherited Astonley. It was like something out of a fairy tale."

"Was it really so bad—before?" asked Marion, touched.

Tom laughed.

"No. I rubbed along. But it's going to take me a long while to get used to the idea that I don't have to grub round for every pound. You see, I wasn't trained for anything. I never had much education. The dice are weighted against you then. But, look, Marion, you don't want to hear about that."

"I'm interested."

"Really?" his voice was eager. "Oh hell! this is no time to talk to you about this, with poor Bella not yet buried, but I'm dead scared you'll have left Astonley before I get my say in."

Suddenly Marion knew what he was trying to tell her. Inexplicably, she wished that he wouldn't.

"Tom, you don't have to—"

"But I want to," he broke in, "Look, about Bella. I met her on the boat. I guess I was kind of excited about everything and I got a bit carried away. Fancy me getting involved in a shipboard romance! Then I came here, and I began to wonder how Bella would fit it at Astonley. It wasn't difficult to see that she would not. That's why I didn't mention her at first. I didn't know what to do. I was half hoping that Bella might have had second thoughts, too, but she hadn't, and I hadn't the nerve to tell her I didn't love her. You see, Marion, I had met you. Either way, I was going to lose you. If I married Bella, that would be that. And if I jilted her, you'd think I was just a load of manure. So I thought I had better go ahead with it, and maybe, when Bella got here she wouldn't want to stay. But I'll admit I was glad that she decided to have her Scottish holiday first. It would give me time to pull myself together."

He lapsed into silence. Marion could think of nothing to say in reply. Every phrase which formed in her mind seemed to be wrong. Above all, she did not want to hurt him.

"Tom, I don't know what to say," she admitted at last.

"You don't have to say anything," he assured her. "I'm told you thought the world of my cousin James, and he treated you like dirt. It would take a long time for a girl like you to get over that. I don't want to rush you. I promise you I won't speak of this again until you give me permission."

They swept up the short drive to the Dower House. The lights in the downstairs rooms were blazing.

Marion slipped out of the car.

"Are you coming in?"

Tom shook his head.

"I don't want to push my luck too far. You know me and Roderick. We don't want another family row tonight. But, Marion, see if you can persuade Rosalie. I don't want you to leave Astonley."

CHAPTER 17

BELLA MANSTON'S friend was a smartly turned out woman, with carefully dyed hair, impeccable make-up and a pair of the hardest, shrewdest eyes that Charles Warren had ever seen.

"I wanted to have a word with you about Mrs Manston, Miss . . . er . . . ?"

"Courtney. And it's Mrs. I'm a widow."

Instantly, Charles doubted the existence of the husband. He had met such "widows" before. Mrs Courtney seemed to be a prime example of the type. He wondered why Bella Manston had chosen to make a friend of her. Like calling to like?

She was weighing him up. She appeared to be satisfied with her investigation, for a smile flashed at him.

"I'm sure I'll be delighted to help you, Mr Warren."

"I feel I would like to know more about Mrs Manston," he said easily, "What sort of a person she was. Had you known her long?"

Mrs Courtney shook her head.

"No," she admitted regretfully, "Only since she came to the hotel. A week last Monday that was. It was her first trip to Europe. Someone had recommended this hotel to her, so she made a booking here. She came here straight off the boat."

"She didn't know any of the other guests?"

"No. She was all on her own, and I think she felt in need

of a sympathetic listener. She thought she had been taken in, and she was real mad about it."

"Taken in? Who by?"

"Thomas Winter, of course. It seems he hadn't turned up at a rendezvous they had made for when they were through Customs. Of course, Bella leapt to the very worst conclusion. She didn't admit it, but I think she had been a little bit foolish on board that ship. People do get carried away, I'm told. And there are men who will promise a girl anything, just to get all she can offer, and then fade away when it comes to the pay-off."

"Would you have said that Bella was the sort of woman to be 'foolish'?"

Mrs Courtney laughed.

"Not in the normal way of things. I'd have said she was a most sensible girl."

Charles could imagine what Mrs Courtney's definition of that might be: no favours without a substantial down payment or even the altar itself.

"So Bella thought she had been had. And she was mad about it. What was she proposing to do about it? Write it off to experience?"

"Hardly," retorted Mrs Courtney. "He had told her all about this place, Astonley, but by that time she didn't believe a word of it. But she said it was worth while doing a bit of checking up."

"What did she do?"

"I don't know, quite. But she went away for a night."

"What day was that?"

"Wednesday. She was back here on Thursday."

"Do you know where she went?"

"No. But she was pretty pleased with herself when she came back. Then he phoned her on Thursday night, and that put her on top of the world. He said he had misunderstood the arrangement for meeting her and had waited the Lord knows how long for her somewhere else. It sounded a bit of a tale to me, but what did it matter? They were engaged and it was all plain sailing. Or so she thought, poor soul. She was that thrilled when his letter came. I think she had been regretting that she had promised to go to Scotland with those other folks—people she had met on the boat, I believe—but Tom had told her that things were a bit sticky at Astonley, with the family, and it would be better to give them a week or two to get used to the idea."

"Do you know how long she was intending to stay at Astonley?"

"For ever, I should think," Mrs Courtney was surprised at the question, "She took all her things with her."

"So, in fact, if her body hadn't been found, she could have just disappeared? Would you, for instance, have thought to ask questions if you hadn't heard from her?"

"Well, no. I'll admit," she went on confidentially, "I'll admit that I was half hoping that she would suggest that I should go up and stay with her, when she was settled, but it wasn't as though we were close friends. Ships in the night, and all that." She looked at him from under her lashes. "Are you married, Mr Warren?"

Charles assured her that he was and made his escape.

He returned to his office, reflecting that he had virtually wasted half the morning. He doubted if they would ever learn more about Bella Manston. He was toying with the idea of sending through an inquiry to the United States when Inspector Morton came on the line.

He sounded faintly jubilant.

"I've a line on Roderick Winter," he said, "It's through that nurse, Nora Deeping. Those two are having an affair. They have kept it very quiet. No one at Astonley seems to have a clue about it, not even the Lightfoot woman, the housekeeper, who is one of the world's prime snoopers. But

Roderick has a friend who has a cottage near Matlock. He was staying there at the time when James Winter's house was broken into. Or so he says. And you can bet your boots that nurse was there with him. It wouldn't have been the first time. They have been using it regularly."

"It wouldn't be too far to drive from there to London and back in the same day," Charles agreed, "It would be interesting to know if that rag and bone man could identify Nurse Deeping as the fair woman he saw that afternoon."

"Wouldn't it just?" sighed Morton, "But we haven't a hope of that until we have enough evidence to persuade Superintendent Beech that it is worth looking into. But, you know, Mr Warren, they could have worked the whole thing between them. She would have had to send off the anonymous letter, and remember she did have a copy of the evening newspaper. Marion Loring found it. They could have worked the break-in between them. And Roderick could have sent off the telegram. Come to think of it: who would be the most likely person to know if another bad shock would finish the old man off? The nurse, every time."

"Where is she now?"

"Gone back to London. She left Astonley on Sunday morning. She told everyone she would be at home for a fortnight, having a little holiday."

Charles laughed.

"I can imagine what you want me to do, Inspector. All right, let's have her address. I'll go round and see her."

But before he could set out for Nora's house, his secretary brought in a bulky envelope. Charles took one look at the contents and hastened to his chief's office.

"The information on the post office clerk has come through from the police."

Liston glanced through the papers which Charles handed to him. They were photostats of typed sheets.

"Benjamin Price," Liston commented, "is quite a lad. But is he the one we want? He's younger. Thirty or thereabouts. Wait a minute, it says here that he was trained in the post office but hasn't worked there for a long time. Not since he found ways of making easy money. They have been looking for him since the end of April in connection with a robbery. What else? Oh, yes, can't keep his hands off the girls." He looked up. "What do you think, Charles? Is he the one we want?"

"Take a look at the photograph they enclose."

"Not very flattering," Liston muttered, examining it, "but painfully clear. Here, I have seen this before. Or something very like it."

"People look different when they are dead."

"Good heavens! That corpse the French have found. Where is that photograph?"

"I've sent down for it."

Liston rang for his secretary. Five minutes later they were comparing the two pictures.

"No mistake about it," Liston decided, "even allowing for the fact that the chap has been strangled. Interesting. Even more so, if he happens to be our man as well."

"Exactly," said Charles grimly, "We have all ruled out Thomas Winter because he was in America when the crimes were committed. And there wasn't a smell of an accomplice. But this fellow, Ben Price, comes from Bristol. So does Tom Winter. Price was in London. He could have done all the dirty work. Then he disappeared quietly, over to France, to wait for his share in the gains."

"Then he got more than he bargained for," Liston commented, "But is this any more than an interesting theory, Charles?"

"Of all the people at Astonley, the only one who was abroad when this chap was killed—Tuesday, in fact—was Thomas Winter."

"But what about the Manston woman. She was killed on Monday."

"So she was. That is a bit of a snag, I admit. Unless that murder was a bit of private enterprise by someone else at Astonley. We can soon check if Tom Winter crossed back to England again to finish her off, then rushed back to do in his pal. I'll set that going, then I'll nip down to that post office with these photographs and see if I can get a positive identification."

It was a great disappointment.

"It's a bit like him," one of the women said helpfully, "But it's definitely not him. Mr Price had greyish hair and he wore glasses too. Those with heavy, thick, black rims."

"A little powder can turn hair grey. Try to imagine that photograph with spectacles."

But the woman shook her head.

"No. I'm sorry. It isn't him. There's that dimple in the middle of his chin. You couldn't mistake that. Mr Price definitely didn't have one."

There was no choice but accept it. Charles thanked the woman and left. As he passed through the office a thought struck him: there were several very pretty girls about. If it had been the right Ben Price, someone would have commented on his hanging round them. According to the Bristol police, girls were Price's great weakness.

It was worth checking up. Charles turned back to his informant.

"Dear me, no," she laughed in response to his question, "Quite the reverse. Mr Price was very quiet. I don't think he even noticed the girls."

So that was that. It was not beyond the bounds of possibility that there were two men of the name of Benjamin Price.

Charles left the post office.

It was a very unsatisfactory situation. He had merely

wasted time, his own and other people's. He was no nearer to finding the post office clerk. He doubted if he was worth looking for anyway. True, the business of the faked references smelt but there could be a number of explanations for that. And none of them of the slightest interest to him.

As for the other Ben Price, now stiff in a French mortuary, he was of interest solely to the police. Not that they would be greatly concerned now that he was dead.

Unless. . . .

The sudden thought was like a ray of sunlight in the gloom. Perhaps he had only wasted half his time after all. Ben Price had crossed to France somehow. He might have gone in the ordinary way, but it was more likely that he had travelled by an underworld route—and those things were very much the concern of the Ministry. It would be useful to know which route was in favour at the moment. . . .

More happily, Charles took himself off to the docks, to have a word or two with his contacts there.

A couple of hours later he struck oil.

He was on board the s.s. *Harry of Lancaster*, a vessel which spent the entire summer season carrying loads of trippers over to France for the day. The captain, an old acquaintance, had greeted him warily, a circumstance which aroused Charles's interest.

"I've been wondering whether I ought to contact you, Mr Warren," his host said suddenly.

"Oh? Why?"

"Just an odd thing which happened a few days ago. The devil of it is I haven't anything concrete to offer you. But you remember what we were talking about a few months ago?"

Charles nodded.

"That's what I'm checking up on today. The big difficulty about France from the escaper's point of view is that a man must have papers there, but if that can be overcome it's easy enough to get into France. And your ships offer a very simple way. Either as a passenger, who makes the journey one way only, or by posing as a member of the crew."

"Aye," the captain added, "and with all the temporary men we take on for the season, that's only too easy."

"So what's up? You think your ship may have been used?"

"I do. Though I may be wrong. But I've been keeping a sharp look-out since we last spoke about it."

"Have you lost a passenger?"

"No. If this fellow was slipping across, he did it as a member of the crew. The trouble is, I only caught a glimpse of him, and I was too far away from him to have him stopped."

On an impulse, Charles pulled out the photograph of Ben Price.

"Not this man by any chance?"

The captain looked at it for a long time.

"I don't really know," he said at last, reluctantly, "It could have been. That's as near as I can go. But I didn't see him close to."

"When was this?"

"I can tell you that all right. It was last Tuesday, on the morning crossing to Boulogne."

Charles went back to Whitehall more than satisfied. The matter of Ben Price was neatly tied up. He had died within hours of landing in France. Where he had been since April, when he had disappeared from Bristol, was strictly no concern of his.

His secretary informed him brightly that the Oldchurch police had checked Thomas Winter's passport. No sign that he had made a hasty trip back to England on Sunday or Monday.

"Do you want us to do any more, sir?"

Charles shook his head.

"No. Leave it. We can forget that now. I'm going out again. Will you let Mr Liston know that I am going to see that nurse."

But there he drew another blank. Nora Deeping was not at home. Her family had not seen her for several weeks.

Charles phoned the news through to Oldchurch.

"I don't know that I like the sound of that," Inspector Morton commented thoughtfully, "She was last seen driving off with Roderick Winter to catch the London train. Murderer's accomplices have a habit of winding up dead."

CHAPTER 18

MARION took the field path from the Dower House to Astonley itself. It was shorter than the road, and this was just the morning for a stroll. The good weather had returned and with it the old peace and security. Or so it seemed to Marion. It was difficult to recall that only two days ago she had been dragged off to London by Superintendent Beech and then, reluctantly, released. Since then there had been no word from the police, and she dared to breathe freely again. She hoped that they had come to their senses at last.

It was inconceivable that anyone here could be the murderer.

Or was it?

The thought had spoilt the morning. Now she hastened down the path. A moment later Astonley lay before her, but she did not stop to admire its beauty.

A voice called to her as she crossed the terrace.

"Marion! What are you doing here?"

She swung round. Roderick, his face full of mischief, was lounging against the wall.

"You're out of luck," he went on, grinning, "Tom's not here."

Marion felt her colour rising.

"I came to fetch some things I had forgotten," she explained, hoping she sounded dignified.

"Forgotten?" he drawled.

The trouble was there might be an element of truth in

the jibe. Marion was honest enough to admit that to herself. She didn't *have* to fetch those things this morning. Any time would do. But she had seen nothing of Tom since he had met her at the station and brought her home.

Trust Roderick to see too much!

She passed him without another word and went into the house. He followed her.

"What do you want here, anyway?" she demanded, goaded.

Roderick laughed.

"Just keeping out of Mother's way. I'm sick of doing jobs round the place. What a fuss you women make about moving house."

"There is a lot to be done."

A sulky expression crept over Roderick's face.

"I never knew Mother could be so pig-headed. Can't you do anything with her?"

"The decision is hers. I think Tom genuinely wants her to reconsider. Perhaps if we could get him to talk to her himself."

Roderick brightened.

"It's a thought."

They strolled into the hall. It was all so unchanged, so unchangeable. Marion could not imagine even a different arrangement of the furniture.

Roderick was making for the polished oak table which bore a bright silver tray. On the tray were two or three letters.

"Ah, the mail!" he exclaimed, swooping on it.

"Roderick," Marion protested, "That will be for Tom. Ours came up to the Dower House just before I left."

It did not stop him glancing through the little pile of envelopes.

"There!" he said, extracting the bottom one, "That's for me. You know how the post gets jumbled up."

He flourished the letter in front of her eyes.

Marion knew the answer to that one. She sighed in exasperation.

"Uncle Robert never minded you using this address instead of the Dower House," she pointed out, "but Tom may have different ideas. If I were you I'd lay off it."

"If I were you," he mimicked, "And, of course, you know all about Tom, don't you, dear?"

"Don't be an idiot."

"You're blushing, Marion."

Her cheeks were hot and there was nothing she could do about it.

"I'm not blaming you," Roderick was saying, "Most girls would put up with a lot for the sake of a place like this. And I dare say Tom would be a damn sight kinder to you than our late, lamented James."

"I don't want to talk about it," she said furiously, "Not that there is anything to discuss."

"No?"

"No," she echoed firmly, "Anyway, it's not decent, with poor Bella Manston not yet buried."

Roderick snorted.

"If Tom has any sense he'll soon realise he is well out of that."

"What do you mean?"

"Don't tell me you haven't cottoned on to the sort Bella was."

"What was she?"

"A harpy. A hard-faced bitch who would lead a man a hell of a life. I can't imagine how a chap like Tom could get mixed up with her, much less offer her marriage."

Marion could have told him. It struck her that she had only half believed Tom's explanation the other night. But this made sense of it. She hadn't wanted to conclude that Tom must be a bit of a ladies' man. He had sounded so sincere. Part of her had wanted to believe him utterly.

She felt a sudden rush of affection for Roderick, and was moved to confide in him.

"Roderick, who is it? Which of us is it? The murderer."

To her surprise he laughed.

"So at last you are coming round to looking facts in the face, Marion."

"I don't understand."

"Come off it, Marion. Use your loaf. You, of all people, should be thinking your head off. You aren't a half-wit, though anyone might think that you were from the way you've been letting the police trample all over you."

"But I don't see that my thinking about it can do any good. I don't know anything."

"I'll bet you do, all the same. Look, it isn't as though there is a wide choice of suspects."

"But how—"

"It isn't *how* that's important," he broke in, "it's *why*."

"Why?"

"Motive. *How* it was done can be worked out afterwards. So what have we got? You, for a start. We know all about your possible motive. Own back on James. Fair enough, if you did. He deserved it."

Marion stared at him in consternation. Just how much did Roderick know?

"But I can't see you taking it out on Uncle Robert, too," he swept on, "After all, you could have hurt him terribly by *telling* him, couldn't you?"

"Yes," agreed Marion in a daze.

"But you didn't." Roderick acknowledged her admission by a flicker of a smile. "So that rules you out. Who's next. Here we come to the interesting bit. The money. And Astonley. James was the direct heir. If Uncle Robert had been killed first, James would have inherited. Kill him off next and there are double death-duties to pay. That would never do. Much cheaper to do it the other way round. Not to mention easier."

"But, Roderick, *you*?"

He grinned at her.

"This isn't a confession. I'm just pointing out the obvious. Everyone thought I was next in line. Tom's arrival was one hell of a shock all round. Only—I didn't do it. As I see it, there are only two people left. My mother and—"

"Your mother? Roderick, you must be crazy."

"Why shouldn't it be her? With a bit of help, of course. And I could give you a fair idea of where that might come from, too. She's been aching to get away from this place for years, only Grandpa threatened to stop her allowance if she did. Now that he is dead she can go and live where she likes."

"How you can even think such a thing of your own mother is beyond me," Marion exclaimed.

He was laughing at her again.

"If you don't fancy her as a murderess, how about the other person?"

"Who?"

"A pal of yours. David."

"David?"

"Yes, no one ever thinks about him, do they? There he is, always about the place. It's his job. He has to be. He comes and goes as he pleases, and no one takes any notice. He's almost a part of the scenery. But I've got my eye on him. I'm doing a nice little line of investigation all of my own."

"Roderick, stop! All right, suppose David wanted to get hold of the money Uncle Robert left him, though I don't believe a word of it myself. But why should he go to all that elaborate business of killing James, and Alice, too?"

"The money Grandpa left him? I'm not talking about that, Marion. No, Astonley." He paused to stare at her for a moment. "Didn't you realise that David is next in line after me?"

"Is he?"

"He is. The place is entailed to pass in the male line. You can take it from me, David is the next one."

The world seemed to have stopped turning. Marion could only stare at Roderick.

"I know he has always been a friend of yours, Marion," he went on more quietly, "But what do you really know about him?"

"I don't know," she admitted, shaken, "I've always taken him for granted. He is—just David."

"He's a human being, with failings, like the rest of us." Roderick glanced round. "You know, I can understand a man being willing to kill to get hold of a place like this. And I'm not the grandson of a belted earl who has had the unpleasant experience of being jilted by his girl-friend because the said earl went bankrupt and had to sell up."

"David?" gasped Marion.

Roderick nodded.

"Didn't you know? Of course, it was years ago. When David was twenty. He was all but engaged to the girl. It was due to be announced at his twenty-first. Then the plug was pulled out of the family fortunes, and that was that. The engagement went down the drain too."

"Who was she?" asked Marion through stiff lips.

"Funny. She ended up marrying our worthy Doctor Ludlow. Fascinating woman, the lovely Flora. Don't you remember her?"

"Of course I do." Marion was struggling hard to maintain a grasp on the point at issue while her imagination was trying to whirl her off into some appalling emotional storm. "But, look here, Rod, if all that happened years ago, why should David start murdering now to get hold of Astonley?"

Roderick shrugged.

"Perhaps he's thinking of getting married and doesn't intend to be caught out a second time. However it is, if he is the joker in the pack, Tom and I had better watch out."

Marion was sure that, if her mind were only to clear, she could pick a dozen holes in the argument. But her head was spinning. Her one desire was to get away.

Roderick turned back to fiddle with the mail remaining on the table.

"Here, what's this?"

In spite of herself, Marion turned to look.

"French postmark," muttered Roderick, "And perfumed," he added, sniffing the envelope.

"Roderick, you do pry!"

He grinned at her.

"Why not? I like it. Your trouble is that you don't notice things until they are thrust right under your nose."

"Like you and Nora Deeping?" she retorted, stung.

The smile vanished from Roderick's face.

"I can't think what you mean," he said, scrutinising the envelope once more. "Hullo, there's a return address on the back. 'Mademoiselle Janine Rochart, Hotel Plage, Quimper.' " The grin reappeared, "You'd better get your skates on, Marion. It looks as though Tom has picked up another girl-friend."

She knew he was teasing deliberately, to get his own back for the thrust about Nora. But she had had enough. She fled. Behind her she heard him call out, "Ah, Tom, there you are! There is a letter from your new lady-love." But she did not linger. All she wanted was to be alone.

To her relief she met no one on her return to the Dower House, but as she came in sight of the building she caught a glimpse of David's stocky figure in the garden. Marion stopped, her heart thudding.

He disappeared round the side of the house. She waited for a moment, expecting to hear the Land Rover, his usual form of transport, start up. But there was no sound. He must have gone into the house, she decided.

And just at the moment she could not have faced him. She slipped off in the direction of the woods.

It was past noon when she returned to the Dower House. She had wandered down through the woods to the far side of the lake. Across the expanse of water lay the village. She had sat on the bank and quietly watched the quiet tempo of life in Winsmere.

At last, reluctantly, she stood up and started slowly back up the hill.

Someone—a man—was shouting.

Automatically, Marion quickened her pace. The noise had come from the garden, or, maybe, through an open window from the house. She had not been able to distinguish any words, but it had been a cry of urgency.

Now all was quiet again. Ominously quiet.

She ran through the garden and into the house by the side door. She met no one, but she could hear a voice in the hall. Tom's voice.

"Yes, Inspector," he was saying, and Marion realised that he was on the phone, "Come at once. To the Dower House. I've phoned Dr Ludlow, but there's nothing he can do. Roderick's dead."

CHAPTER 19

IN WHAT seemed like no time at all, although in fact it was a matter of some hours, Superintendent Beech was with them, deposited by a helicopter which touched down on the lawn.

From her bedroom window, Marion watched him arrive and shuddered.

Inspector Morton emerged from the house to greet his superior. The girl would have been surprised to know that he welcomed the arrival of the Scotland Yard man with an equal lack of enthusiasm.

"Hard luck, Inspector," Beech proceeded to rub salt into the wound at once, "having your prime suspect murdered almost in front of your very eyes."

"Yes, sir," Morton replied stolidly.

"You young fellows are all the same," Beech went on complacently, "Always think you know better than the old ones. Now let's see what we've got here."

They went into the house.

"Where did it happen?"

Morton opened a door leading off the hall.

"In here, sir. Roderick Winter called this his Den."

It was a small room, furnished with club armchairs, bookshelves and a desk. A round occasional table held an elaborately cut set of crystal decanters. One was missing.

"The cyanide was in the whisky, sir," Morton explained, "It's gone off to the lab."

Beech nodded.

"Witnesses?"

"Waiting for you, sir. We are using the diningroom for interviews."

Beech allowed Morton to conduct him to the room. He settled himself in a chair.

"Right, wheel the first one in. Who is it?"

"Mr Thomas Winter, sir. He saw it happen."

Thomas was subdued.

"The most shocking thing I ever saw in my life, Superintendent. And I can't help thinking that it could just as easily have been me."

"Tell me, Mr Winter."

"Well, Roderick came over to Astonley this morning. I expect you know that we had a dust-up a few days ago. I was anxious to forget all that, so you can understand I was pleased to see him. And he seemed just as keen as I was to make it up. We chatted for a bit, then he suggested that I go back with him to talk to his mother. About not leaving the Dower House. Naturally, I agreed. So we came over here. Mrs Winter was out, so Roderick took me into his Den for a drink while we waited for her. Rod asked me what I'd have. Lord help me, I asked for a whisky. He poured for both of us."

"But you didn't touch yours?"

"My word, no. I was lighting a cigarette. My lighter was kicking up—wouldn't spark—and I was getting mad with it. Rod offered me a box of matches, then picked up his drink, said 'Cheers!' A couple of seconds later he was writhing on the floor."

"Cyanide is very quick," agreed Beech grimly, and looked at Morton.

"It was in the decanter," said the Inspector, "Lucky for you that you didn't touch your drink, Mr Winter."

"But how did it get in there?"

"That's what we have to find out, Mr Winter," said Beech, "Any suggestions?"

"Hell, no!" Tom exclaimed, "I didn't even know we had any of the stuff in the place. Isn't it what they use for wasps' nests, or something?"

"Yes. I may say, Mr Winter," Morton interposed, "that between your garden shed and your farm stores you have a pretty fine collection of poisons. The cyanide was bought last Monday by the gardener. And for a wasps' nest. In Miss Loring's piece of the garden."

"Here! You aren't going after that poor girl again, are you?"

"It's our job," Beech told him curtly, and indicated that he was finished with him for the time being. "I'll see that gardener next, Inspector."

Bertie Hough was a man with a grievance. He took it as a personal affront that the murderer had pinched his cyanide to do his dirty work.

He glared belligerently at Beech.

"Of course, I bought it on Monday. Signed the book in the chemist's in Oldchurch, too. I had to do it meself, of course. No use waiting for her ladyship to fetch it in."

"I suppose you mean Miss Loring?" asked Beech.

"That's right. Her." Hough sniffed meaningly.

"Did you tell her about the wasps' nest?"

"Of course I did. But did she offer to get the stuff for it? Not likely."

"Did you tell anyone else?"

Hough bridled.

"Why should I tell folks as how I've got wasps' nests in me garden?" he demanded.

"So Miss Loring was the only one who was likely to know that there was a bottle of cyanide in the garden shed. How come you hadn't used it?"

"Too wet," muttered Hough darkly, "And there was I all set to use it today."

"Is the garden shed locked?"

Hough stared.

"Locked? Never in my time, and I've been here getting on for thirty years."

"So anyone could have taken it from the shed?"

"If they knew it was there. I don't encourage folks to come poking round my shed."

"But Miss Loring, since she is a gardener herself, must do," Beech persisted.

Hough suddenly caught on.

"You're barking up the wrong tree, Super," he said. "That woman's a danged nuisance in the garden, but I don't reckon as how she'd go murdering people."

Beech was unmoved by the unexpected tribute.

The gardener went out, slamming the door behind him.

"This is going to be tricky," Beech admitted, "If we are going to make out a case which will stand up in court, that is. How about the bottle the stuff was in?"

"We found it under a shrub the other side of the house. No fingerprints, naturally. Wiped, by the look of it."

"Hum. That's no good. Who's next?"

"The mother. Mrs Rosalie Winter."

Rosalie came in, pale but calm. Morton thought that she was too deeply shocked to break down. He also thought it inadvisable to question her at this time, but she had said that she was willing. He took comfort that the doctor was somewhere round the house, if anything should happen.

Even Beech made an effort to be gentle.

But Rosalie could tell them little.

"I was out. No, the house was not locked up. We don't bother. The servants would be about. And Marion. And Roderick." She closed her eyes for a moment.

"When was the whisky last in use?"

"Yesterday evening. Superintendent, my son was a creature of habit. He didn't drink much, but I could have set a clock by him. One drink before lunch, and again before dinner."

"Whisky?"

"Always. He didn't care for gin. Or cocktails."

"Do you drink whisky?"

"I never touch it. Nor does Marion."

Beech nodded.

"So the poison was intended for him alone. It must have been added to the decanter this morning, in the sure knowledge that it would have done its work by lunch-time."

Rosalie put a hand to her eyes.

"Is there anything else, Superintendent?"

"Not at the moment, madam."

Without a word she left her chair and slipped out of the room.

"What about the servants, Inspector?" asked Beech.

Morton sighed.

"There are two maids, sir. Neither heard nor saw a thing. Useless. Shall I bring them in?"

"Later. Let's have a little think before we tackle the girl."

Marion was halfway down the staircase when Rosalie came out from her interview with the Superintendent. She stopped, halted by the stricken expression on her adoptive aunt's face.

Rosalie crossed the hall like a sleepwalker. She opened the door to the drawingroom.

From inside, Marion heard Dr Ludlow exclaim, "Rosalie!"

She ran lightly down the last few steps, thinking that she

might help. She stopped dead at the open doorway.

Rosalie and Dr Ludlow were clasped in a close embrace.

Marion fled softly down the hall and out through the front door into the garden.

It was no business of hers.

All the same, it was a shock. And a question popped up in her mind. It was no sin to fall in love and they were both free to marry. Why, then, did they keep it a secret?

And David. What about David?

She could hear Roderick's words revolving in her brain: he and Tom would have to watch out. That was only a few hours ago. Now Roderick was dead. And David had been to the Dower House that morning. She had seen him.

But, apparently, no one else had. Marion had made discreet inquiries from the maids. As far as they were concerned they had not set eyes on Mr David.

Again she recalled Roderick's own words: David could go where he pleased on the estate, and no one would think anything of it. Just part of the scenery.

And he would be sure to know about the purchase of the poison for the wasps' nest. Bertie Hough would never have paid for it out of his own pocket. He would have put in a chit for it at the estate office, as he always did with oddments which he bought for the garden. Knowing Hough, the chit would be on David's desk almost before the cyanide was on the shelf in the shed.

She felt sick at heart.

David, of all people!

Somehow it was worse that it should be him.

Marion did not know what to do. Commonsense told her that she should inform the police. But this was about *David*.

It occurred to her that Superintendent Beech would never believe her.

She went back into the house. The hall was empty and

she noted, thankfully, that the drawingroom door was now firmly shut. She crossed to the telephone, dialled quickly and waited impatiently for the series of clicks to end and the ringing tone to tell her that she was through.

At last an impersonal voice announced,

"Ministry of Security."

"I would like to speak to Mr Charles Warren, please."

"I'm afraid Mr Warren isn't in. The Director's office is taking his calls. Will that do?"

Marion sighed, disappointed.

"It will have to, I suppose."

"Who is calling?"

"Miss Loring, from Astonley, Shropshire."

"One moment, please."

It seemed an age, and Marion was in an agony of fear lest Superintendent Beech should swoop down on her before she had completed her call.

Then Liston himself was on the line.

Marion poured it all out, hoping that he would be able to sort out the jumble of facts and fears. All the time she kept an eye on the door to the diningroom. At any minute it could open and her chance would be gone.

"It can't be David," she heard herself saying again and again, "Please help us."

The calm, dry voice at the other end of the line assured her that they would do all they could.

"Charles is on your job now. He's gone to Bristol."

Marion put down the phone.

There was no hope left. A journey to Bristol could only mean one thing: Charles was collecting evidence against David and there was some connection through his sister in Bristol.

"Ah, there you are, Miss Loring," said Inspector Morton.

Marion looked up. She had not heard the door open, but there he was, and behind him Superintendent Beech.

Somebody thundered on the front door with the heavy knocker.

Marion started.

"Just a minute," she said, "I'll see who that it."

While the Inspector waited, she flung open the door, and fell back as a fair girl walked past her into the hall.

"Is it true?" demanded Nora Deeping, "Is it true that Roderick is dead?"

CHAPTER 20

"I'VE been looking for you," exclaimed Inspector Morton. "Where have you been?"

Nora tossed her head.

"What does that matter? Is Roderick dead?"

"Yes, he's dead," said Morton heavily, "You'd better come in and sit down, Miss."

Nora's face was white.

"So they said in Oldchurch. I didn't believe them."

She stumbled forward, and Morton put out a hand to steady her. Nora shook him off.

"I'm all right," she said fiercely, "How did it happen?"

"He was poisoned."

"Who did it?"

"We don't know yet." He gazed at her speculatively. "Maybe we might have a better idea if you answered a few questions."

Nora licked her lips nervously.

"Ask away."

Morton stood aside for her to pass.

"In here, then."

Beech's eyebrows shot up mock surprise.

"Well, well, well, the nurse. And where have you been hiding yourself? Witnesses aren't supposed to disappear, you know. And don't pretend that you've been at home because we know that you haven't."

"I've been staying at a hotel in Stafford."

"And what was the idea behind that?"

Her mouth twisted.

"So that I could keep an eye on Roderick."

Beech's eyebrows shot up in mock surprise.

"So that's the way the wind was blowing, was it?"

"Yes it was," Nora burst out, "You might as well know the lot now. We've been staying in that cottage in Derbyshire every weekend we could get away. But the laugh's on me, Superintendent. Until last Monday I thought he would marry me."

"Just a minute, sir," Morton broke in. He turned to Nora. "Monday? You saw him on Monday?"

"Yes."

"Where?"

"I came over to Oldchurch. He met me outside the station and we drove about for a bit."

"What train did you come on?"

"It arrived at four."

"And did you by any chance notice a woman get off that train? About your own age. Good figure. Red hair. An American accent, if you heard her speak."

Nora stared.

"Why, yes. As a matter of fact I do remember a woman like that. We passed through the ticket barrier together."

Morton could not resist a triumphant glance at Beech.

"That is very interesting," said Beech, but there was an edge to his voice, "Anything else you remember about her?"

Nora shrugged.

"I don't think so. Hey, was she the one that was killed?"

"That's right. You didn't by any chance see who met her off the train?" And Beech returned the Inspector's look.

Nora was silent for a moment.

"It was raining," she said slowly, "I knew Roderick wouldn't come up the drive. He had told me he would wait at the bottom. He didn't want anyone to see us together, the dirty rat. This woman was talkative. We just swopped a few comments about the rain. She was waiting, too. Then a car came up the drive. It didn't come close, but a man got out, and this woman suddenly picked up her bags and went over to him. He met her halfway and took the luggage and they went over to the car."

"A man." Beech's face was a study.

"Yes. I didn't look at him particularly. Medium height, I suppose. There wasn't anything special about him. Oh, yes, he had a beard."

"What colour?"

Nora shrugged.

"Brown, I think. I would have remembered if it had been bright red or something."

"And the car?"

Again Nora was vague.

"I wasn't really interested. I was thinking about having to run down the drive in the rain. It was darkish. A saloon. I don't remember anything else about it."

"And you were with Roderick Winter for the next couple of hours, I suppose?" asked Morton.

Nora nodded.

"Yes. Until the train at six."

The memory did not seem to bring her any pleasure.

"You would have saved us all a great deal of work if you had come forward with this evidence sooner," Morton told her severely.

"But I didn't think it was important. I never realised that I had seen that woman."

Morton just shook his head.

"I told you you were wasting your time on Roderick Winter," said Beech complacently. "Now, young lady, how is it that you have turned up here so opportunely today?"

Nora sighed.

"I couldn't believe that Roderick wanted to finish it all.

I waited in that hotel for days, hoping he would get in touch. Then, this morning, I decided I would come here and have it out with him all over again."

Suddenly the hard, brave mask slipped and the nurse began to cry.

"I should known he would cheat me, somehow," she sobbed.

Marion slipped out of the house as soon as Nora was taken in to see the Superintendent. She knew that she should not go. She had been warned to stay in the house or near it. But she was beyond caring. She could not sit quietly in her room while the world disintegrated.

She had to know.

She had to face David, to look behind the kindly façade which she had accepted as the reality, to see the man beneath.

If she could.

Her resolution faltered when she entered his office, and saw him at his desk, peacefully at his work as if nothing had happened.

"How can you do that at a time like this?" she cried.

David looked up, surprised. He had not heard her come in.

"Why, Marion! Come and sit down. I didn't know you were here. Now, what were you saying? How can I do what?"

She made a gesture towards the desk.

"Work. Fill in the forms, or whatever you are doing."

He smiled.

"The work has to be done sometime. And there are always a lot of forms," he added ruefully.

She was in danger of slipping back into her old attitude. He was more like the Rock of Gibraltar than the shifty, greedy murderer she had been imagining.

"Work takes your mind off troubles," he added soberly. "How is it going at the Dower House?"

Marion shivered.

"Superintendent Beech is there. I haven't seen him yet."

He gazed down at her enigmatically.

"Running away again, Marion?"

She shook her head.

"There is nowhere to run to now."

He turned away abruptly.

"What about your friend, Mr Warren?"

His tone startled her.

"I wouldn't call him a friend," she said defensively.

"You ran to him."

"Only because I thought he might help."

"And did he?"

"I suppose he did. But he brought me straight back here. I don't know what connection he has with the police. It must be something very hush-hush. The Ministry place is like a prison. Guards on all the doors."

David began to pace about the room. Marion watched him in growing alarm. She wondered how she could have imagined that he was his normal self. Or was this frightening stranger the reality she had come to see.

For she was frightened of him now. There was a sense of passionate anger about him which filled her with dread.

"Marion," he said abruptly, "what happened during James's visit here at the end of April?"

The unexpectedness of it took her aback.

He misconstrued her hesitation. In two swift strides he was beside her. His hands shot out and grasped her wrists. He pulled her to her feet and held her.

"Tell me."

"No," she gasped. "David, you're hurting me."

If anything his grip tightened.

"What did he do to you?"

Marion stared up at him. His eyes, not more than eighteen inches from her own, blazed down at her.

His will was too strong for her.

"All right, I'll tell you." She jerked herself free of him as he relaxed for an instant. "If you must know, James made love to me. It was my own fault. It started so innocently, the pair of us sitting at the far side of the garden, talking about old times. At least, James was. And I was thinking that at last I was over it all, and I could meet him and he would mean nothing more to me than any other member of the family. Then suddenly, he started a long tale of how disastrous his marriage was turning out and what a mistake he had made. Like a fool I listened to him. He kissed me. And I let him. I forgot about Alice. I thought I was still in love with him, and there was nothing I would ever be able to do about it. I came to my senses when he started to pull at my clothes. Then I tried to fight him off. But it was too late. I was no match for him."

"Are you telling me he raped you?"

She would not look at him.

"Call it that if you like."

"Did you tell Robert?"

Marion shook her head.

"I was too ashamed. Besides, who would have believed me? James would have said I had been willing. And—" he stopped, her voice drowned in tears.

"And what?" David prompted her harshly.

"I didn't tell you all of it. Afterwards, James laughed at me. He said, 'If that's the best you can do, I'll stick to Alice."

There was a moment's silence, then David said firmly, "I'm glad he's dead."

At the Dower House an agitated constable was explaining to Inspector Morton that Miss Loring had disappeared.

"She can't have gone far, sir."

"She was told to stay here. And it was your job, my lad, to make sure that she did."

The ringing of the phone interrupted them. The constable leapt to answer it as a man to his salvation.

"It's for you, sir," he announced, "Mr Warren calling from Bristol."

Inspector Morton took the call. Then he went back into the diningroom where Beech was waiting impatiently. To the constable's relief no one mentioned Miss Marion Loring again.

CHAPTER 21

IT WOULD be more than a nine days' wonder in Winsmere. They would speak of it for years to come. It was exciting enough when the first helicopter landed at the Dower House, but when, the following morning, another one circled the village, people ran out of their houses to watch. This time it did not go to Astonley. Instead it flipped out of sight behind Sir John Prout's house to land in the paddock at the end of the garden.

Two very weary men climbed out and walked towards the house.

Sir John came out to meet them.

"My dear Charles, this is a surprise. I couldn't believe my ears when the message came through an hour ago."

"I'm sorry we couldn't give you more notice, sir, but we didn't know when we would be ready to come. May I present my chief, Alec Liston?"

Sir John eyed them with open curiosity.

"Delighted," he murmured, shaking hands.

"It's very good of you to let us impose on you like this," said Liston, "I hope you don't mind?"

"Mind?" exclaimed Sir John frankly, "I'm honoured. And, I'll admit, damned curious. But I suppose you can't tell me what all this is about?" he ended wistfully.

Liston smiled.

"I promise you we will tell you the whole thing later. We wanted a conference with the police, but we didn't want to go to the police station in Oldchurch. Nor did we want to go to Astonley. We were after neutral ground, so to speak. Charles suggested your place."

"So this is to do with Astonley?" asked Sir John eagerly.

"It is. And I think we can say that the case is finished. Or will be in a matter of a few hours." Liston broke off and yawned. "Oh, excuse me. We've been up all night."

They went into the house.

"Inspector Morton phoned to say he would be here at ten, with Superintendent Beech," Sir John informed them. "Time for breakfast first, if you feel like it."

Gladly, they followed their host to the small room where a laid table awaited them.

"Do you think we can make it stick?" asked Charles suddenly, anxiously.

Liston shrugged.

"I admit I would be happier with a bit more evidence. We have more than enough to convince Beech that we are right. Even yesterday, when you phoned him and told him what you had got, that was enough. But he has to make it stand up in court."

Sir John listened avidly, his eyes darting from one face to the other.

"I wish I could help," he murmured.

Liston looked at him for a moment, then let out a short laugh.

"You never know." He reached for his briefcase, opened it, and fished out a small photograph, which he handed to his host. "There's our murderer. Recognise him?"

"Yes," said Sir John simply, and amazed his guests.

Charles and Liston exchanged glances.

"Are you sure?" demanded Liston.

Sir John nodded.

"I may be an old man, but I'm very good at faces. And I don't see all that many strangers now. I don't stray far from home these days. That fellow is the scout master—I'm sure I mentioned him to you, Charles—who came here last Easter looking for a place for his summer camp. But I suppose he wasn't. Is it a disguise?"

"Of a sort. Moustache, beard and glasses. Very simple and effective. Ordinary people don't notice things like the shape of the ears unless there is something obviously peculiar about them."

Sir John scrutinised the photograph.

"No," he sighed, "I can't say that I recognise the ears. Look like perfectly ordinary ears to me. I say, is this a passport photograph?"

"That's very astute of you, sir," said Liston, "That's just what it is. Now, about this so-called scout master. You remember him quite well?"

"Yes indeed. Very agreeable fellow I thought him at the time."

"Did he ask you questions about the village?"

Sir John thought about it.

"I suppose he did in a way. I met him down in the 'White Swan', you know."

"Did he mention Astonley?"

"I'm sure he did. I remember telling him about the Winters. Is that what he had come to find out?"

"Almost certainly."

"And I told him. I talk too much, and that's the truth," said Sir John dismally.

"If he hadn't had it from you he'd have found someone else to tell him," Liston comforted him, "And we might not have been able to find that person. Your evidence could be very important, Sir John. You see, we had to find a link-up with this village before the whole thing began. You have provided it."

"But who is he?" asked a bewildered Sir John.

Superintendent Beech and Inspector Morton arrived.

Sir John offered them the use of his study, ushered them in, then nobly withdrew to pace round and round the garden, cudgelling his unwilling brains to answer his own question.

"I don't know," began Beech ominously, "that I like the way the Ministry of Security has taken a hand in this case, which, as far as I can see, is nothing to do with them."

Morton looked gloomily at Charles. It was not an auspicious opening.

Alec Liston did not turn a hair.

"Ah, but you see, Superintendent, the corpse was ours."

"Which corpse was that?" demanded Beech, momentarily thrown off his stride.

"The one in France. Ben Price."

"Oh, that one," said Beech grudgingly, "Well, what about it?"

"The body was found in a ditch. He had been murdered. There was nothing in the pockets. No means of identification, except the clothing and an old scar on the abdomen. That scar has been useful in confirming the identity of the corpse, but the important thing is the clothing. That pointed to a British or American origin. That is why the details were forwarded to us. Corpses like that, in circumstances like that, very often turn out to be clients of ours."

Beech grunted. It was as near as he would go to acknowledging the truth of that last statement.

"Now it so happened that we were interested in a certain post office clerk by the name of Ben Price. I won't go into the details of why we were looking for him," Liston went on smoothly, glossing over the fact that in that respect it might be argued that the Superintendent had genuine grounds for his complaint of interference, "We knew that there was something fishy about him. He had had to give references to get his job in the post office. When we traced them we found the addresses to be accommodation ones. The inference is that he wrote his own. Which satisfied the post office. They would never think of checking on the actual addresses. Anyway, that is all a side issue at the moment, though there is a link-up later."

"So you were looking for Ben Price," said Beech, "And he turned up dead in France."

Liston shook his head.

"It wasn't as simple as that. True, we sent out a routine enquiry, and your colleagues in Bristol picked it up. They were looking for a Ben Price, too. It turned out that there were two Ben Prices. And the one in the French morgue was theirs. So we were still looking for ours."

"I don't see," Beech interrupted, "that this is getting us anywhere."

"That is what we thought at the time," Liston agreed amicably, "The next bit is what I can only describe as the luck of the draw. Although we were not concerned with the corpse in Boulogne for its own sake, we were interested in how he had crossed to France. We were assuming that he had used some illegal method, and, in fact, we found one. Via the day tripper boats. More, we turned up a witness who had suspicions that the method had been tried, and on the very day that Price was killed. We did a quick check with the Passport Office. Ben Price had never applied for a passport. So we felt we hadn't wasted our time. We might not have found the Ben Price we were looking for, but we had found another possible escape route we could keep an eye on."

"And block it, sharpish," added Beech, interested in spite of himself.

Liston laughed.

"Not a bit of it. The bright boys would only think up something else in its place—and we would have to start looking all over again."

Beech glared. That attitude was just typical of these counter-espionage blokes. As a good policeman, it riled him.

"The thing which interested us," Liston went on, ignoring the black look, "was whether Ben Price had thought that one up for himself or if he had had help. Now the Bristol police had been looking for Price since the beginning of April. He turned up dead towards the end of June. No one knew where he had been in the meantime. So, to answer your question, there was only one place to start: Bristol. Mr Warren went there yesterday." He glanced at Charles. "Perhaps you would like to take the story up from there."

"Ben Price wasn't difficult to trace. Nor his associates," Charles began, "but I hadn't been talking to his old landlady for more than ten minutes before I realised that I was being given the answers to some of the problems which were troubling you, Superintendent. Strictly speaking," he went on with an ingenuous smile, "I should have phoned you straight away, but we have a discipline in our Service. My immediate reaction was to telephone my chief."

"And I told him that you had been called to Shropshire again, over another murder. Therefore, I instructed Mr Warren to carry on with the investigation. You were obviously snowed under with work, and it was imperative that this murderer should be caught before he could do any further damage."

Inspector Morton gazed at them with admiration. They were a right pair, Alec Liston and Charles Warren. The way they could put it over on Superintendent Beech was a pleasure to listen to. Even he could hardly object or complain of interference when it was put this way. And at most, as he very well knew, it was only half a truth. Once they had their teeth in a problem they would solve it, police or no police.

He reflected that it would need a bigger man than Beech to take on Alec Liston in a departmental war—with any hope of winning.

He hid a smile.

The Superintendent seemed to have lost some of his stuffing. He slumped in his chair.

"And you've got it for me, Mr Warren?"

Charles extracted a file from the briefcase lying open on the table before them.

"Here it is, Superintendent. Of course what put me on to it was the address which Ben Price had given to his landlady for forwarding his letters when he sneaked out of Bristol in April. A London address. I recognised it immediately. It was the same as one of those which the other Ben Price had given as the address of a referee when he was applying for the post office job."

"We checked it," Liston put in, "It's the sort of place where they have weak memories, as you might expect, but we put a bit of pressure on them. We couldn't get a description of the person who had collected the letter taking up the reference—there was only one of those anyway—but they did come forth with a description of the man who had collected several letters for Ben Price. Unfortunately, we hadn't a picture for a visual check, but it sounded remarkably like the man who had worked at that post office. So we had a link-up between our two Ben Prices. And plenty of food for thought."

"And the rest of it?" asked Beech.

Charles tapped the file.

"All in there for you."

"We suggest," Liston put in smoothly, "that you would like to study this for a while. We will rejoin Sir John. Call us when you want us."

Beech eyed the file.

"I suppose you will want to come to Astonley with us, Mr Liston."

Liston's eyebrows rose in pained surprise.

"By no means, Superintendent. It would be most improper for us to appear in your investigation," he said, retreating into a favourite pose, that of the ultra-correct Civil Servant.

Morton was hard put not to laugh outright.

Half an hour later, the two policemen were in the hall, exchanging a few parting words with Sir John and the two men from Whitehall.

"A very neat piece of work, Mr Liston," said Beech with a sour face. "Very neat indeed. Of course, we would have got it ourselves in the end. It was only the luck of that French enquiry coming straight to you that gave you the short cut."

The sheer effrontery of it left even Alec Liston gasping.

CHAPTER 22

MARION was walking in the walled garden with Tom. The beds were ablaze with flowers, the lawn was green velvet, the sun shone down on them and there was a faint humming of bees. Behind them, Astonley, its ancient walls garlanded the length of the terrace with the delicate pink blooms of a climbing rose, slept on, undisturbed by the violence of the past days.

"What will Rosalie do now?" Tom was asking.

"I don't know," Marion replied, "It's rather awful. She is so quiet and self-contained. I'm sure I should want to cry and carry on. But not Aunt Rosalie. Not even when she is alone. You can tell when people have been crying. The way she is at the moment, I wouldn't even dare ask her if she had made any plans. It's almost as if she *knew* something was going to happen to Roderick."

"Don't say that!" Tom exclaimed. "Don't even think it."

Marion sighed. In a way, she wished that she could believe that Aunt Rosalie—aided and abetted by Dr Ludlow, no doubt—was the murderer. But yesterday, David had virtually confessed to it. The remembrance of that moment was breaking her heart.

"I'm going back to France as soon as I can," Tom went on.

Marion put out her hand to him impulsively.

"Oh, don't say all this has made you hate Astonley."

Eagerly he took her hand and held it.

"It hasn't. You know that. But things must be allowed to settle. It will be better, easier for all of you, if I am away from here. But I'll be back, Marion. I'd come back from the end of the world—for you."

Gently she disengaged her hand. She did not want to hurt him. And maybe . . . sometime. . . .

"Don't let's talk about that, Tom. Not just yet."

His eyes smiled into hers.

"Not until you are ready, Marion."

There was a clatter of feet on the flags of the terrace. Almost with relief, Marion swung round.

"Oh !" she gasped and was thankful when Tom took her hand again and held it in a firm, reassuring clasp.

Superintendent Beech and Inspector Morton were standing there.

Waiting for—her?

Tom muttered, "Come on. Let's get it over. I won't let them do anything to you."

He set out towards the policemen, pulling her along behind him.

"Just a word or two, Mr Winter," said Beech grimly, "Miss Loring—"

"Miss Loring stays with me," Tom interrupted firmly, "Anything you have to say can be said to both of us."

The Superintendent did not reply, but apparently accepted the arrangement. They all went into the room which had been Robert Winter's study.

Beech heaved his large form into the chair behind the desk.

"Actually, it was you I wanted a word with, Mr Winter," he began, "I wanted to ask you when you last saw your friend Ben Price."

"Ben Price?"

Beech nodded.

"That's right. Your pal from your Bristol days."

A wary look crept into Tom's eyes.

"I couldn't rightly say, Superintendent. I haven't seen him for quite a long time."

"I'm sure you could do better than that if you tried, Mr Winter."

"Is Ben in trouble again, Superintendent?"

"You could call it that. He's dead."

"Dead?"

"Yes."

Tom's face cleared.

"Then I don't mind telling you, Superintendent," he said frankly. 'I thought you were trying to catch him through me. I don't believe in breaking the law, but I'm a good friend, too. If you follow me, Superintendent."

"You know the Bristol police were looking for him in connection with a robbery?"

"Yes," said Tom heavily, "he told me."

"But you didn't think of informing the police?"

Tom shrugged.

"He was my friend. The police could do their own dirty work. Ben said he was innocent, and I believed him."

"Did you help him to lie low?"

"He didn't need my help. He said he was going to London."

"And you haven't seen him since?"

"Well, yes, as a matter of fact, I have. I was in Bristol recently for a funeral. I saw him that night. But I don't know where he went then."

Beech began tapping his fingers on the top of the desk. To Marion's fascinated gaze they looked like a bunch of animated sausages.

"I wonder if I might trouble you for your passport, Mr Winter," he said thoughtfully, "Just for a quick look at it."

"Look as much as you like, Superintendent. I'll fetch it for you."

"If you don't mind. Inspector, go with him, please."

Tom went without another word or a backward glance at the detective at his heels.

Marion stared wildly at Superintendent Beech.

"What is all this about?"

"If I were you, Miss," he said, not unkindly, "I'd clear out of here. It's going to be a bit unpleasant in a minute."

Marion fled.

At the Dower House, Geoffrey Ludlow was staring down at his patient. There was a look of baffled misery in his eyes.

"For heaven's sake, Rosalie!" he burst out.

She might not have heard him. She sat in her chair as if frozen, staring out of the nearby window.

"Rosalie, you will have to snap out of this. You will end up in a mental home if you go on like this."

She turned her head at that.

"Geoffrey, don't distress yourself. I shall be gone from here soon and you can forget all about me."

"Don't talk rubbish. I love you, Rosalie. How often do I have to tell you?"

"But do you love me, Geoffrey? Or are you telling yourself as well as me? Could you love anyone after the way you loved Flora?"

She surprised him into a laugh.

"Is that what has been bothering you? Obviously, I should have disabused you of that idea years ago. My God! I had been wanting you for years before she died."

"But I don't understand. Flora was so beautiful, and intelligent, and fascinating."

"And a selfish little bitch," he added grimly.

Rosalie could only stare at him.

"I thought you were mad about her."

"I was. At first. Until I discovered what she was. She

was a disappointed woman, was Flora. She married me on the rebound from the breaking of her engagement. Afterwards she wished she hadn't, but she had the sense to keep quiet about it, so no one ever suspected. But I think," he went on, watching her closely, "I think it would have been better if we had not been quite so successful in deceiving everyone."

Rosalie nodded.

"Poor David has never stopped loving her."

Dr Ludlow snorted.

"He doesn't know what a narrow escape he had. She didn't care for him, either. Only for darling Flora. And I suppose you would have married me years ago if you had known the truth?"

The ice had melted. Rosalie was blushing.

"Well, a couple of years ago," she admitted.

He gazed down at her in loving exasperation.

"Then why the devil have we been carrying on a hole-and-corner love affair? Rosalie, you've no idea how I have hated it, but I couldn't do without you. So you weren't afraid of old Robert cutting you and Roderick out of his will?"

She stared at him.

"Did you think that? My dear, what do I care about Robert's money? No, I thought I was just being a bit of comfort to you. I didn't expect you to marry me. And as for Roderick—" she stopped as the tears suddenly began to run down her cheeks.

Dr Ludlow stooped and lifted her into his arms.

"Cry, my darling, you need to. And I'm here to make an honest woman of you as soon as I can get the licence."

Rosalie raised no objections.

Superintendent Beech laid the passport back on the desk. "When did you shave off your beard, Mr Winter?"

Tom shrugged.

"Ages ago. If it is any business of yours."

"It makes quite a difference to your appearance."

"Naturally," Tom commented dryly.

"So much so," Beech went on as if he had not spoken, "that a casual acquaintance wouldn't recognise you. The thing that interests me about your beard is not so much when you shaved it off as when you grew it."

"What are you getting at?" Tom demanded loudly.

There was a short silence, while Tom's glance darted from Beech to Morton and back again.

"Where is Miss Loring?" he asked, modulating his voice back to normal.

"I sent her away," Beech told him, "Now, Mr Winter, this passport was issued to you last April. Had you got your beard then?"

Tom attempted a smile.

"Well, no, actually, I used old photographs."

"Did you? Then how do you account for the fact that we have been able to obtain a copy of this passport photograph of yours from the photographer who took it? *Last April.*"

"There's some mistake."

Beech shook his head.

"Not this time. That photographer keeps negatives for six months only. Then he destroys them. So you were wearing a beard last April, Mr Winter, but the odd thing is that your landlady swears that you were cleanshaven. How about that?"

"Look, Superintendent, I admit that beard was a false one. I rather fancied myself in a beard and I thought I would grow one while I was in the States. But I didn't want to go through the horrible stages of just looking bristly, so I wore a false one. That's all there was to it."

"It won't wash," said Beech in a suddenly hard voice.

"That passport photograph was a risk you had to take. Amongst others. And it backfired on you. I put it to you that the whole idea of the beard dates back a couple of years to a Christmas entertainment put on by the members of a club to which you belonged. Your landlady was most talkative on the subject."

Tom was staring at him.

"You must be off your nut, Superintendent."

"We'll see about that. The point is that Ben Price was also a member of that club and the two of you did a double act. Brought the house down with it. And it was all based on mistaken identity. You both wore beards and moustaches, parted your hair the same way and no one could tell you apart. You were both the same height, colouring and general shape. The simple disguise did the rest."

"All right, so we did a comedy turn. What about it?"

"Ben Price came to you last April. He was in a mess. The police were after him for complicity in a robbery. He needed help. It gave you a bright idea."

"I told you. I didn't help him. He didn't ask for it."

Beech bared his teeth in what might have been a grin.

"Who are you trying to kid? Look, a few months previously you had received the surprise of your life. You had a letter from a lawyer in London, name of Walters, asking for proofs of your identity. You supplied them and in return you learnt that you had a family. And a rich one. You had high hopes, but then you heard nothing more. So you decided to help yourself. The main difficulty was the alibi. Ben Price was a gift from the gods. You offered to fix it for him to get out of England for a while. He jumped at it. So you applied for a new passport—yours was well out of date—and supplied a photograph of a man in a beard. Which would do for either you or Ben Price at a push."

"You're barmy."

Beech ignored him.

"So Ben went off to America as you, and you went off to London as him. You weren't afraid that the Bristol police would catch you. You didn't even answer to the normal description of Ben Price. You'd greyed your hair a bit and adopted a pair of glasses with heavy rims. Quite enough of a disguise for your purposes. You got yourself a job at the post office, on the counter. Then you went to work."

Tom interrupted angrily, "What sort of a fairy tale is this?"

"You'll see. You'll be surprised how much we have learnt in the past couple of days. A lot of us have forgotten when we last went to bed, but it has been worth it, Winter. Now, where were we? Ah, yes, the beginning of your plan. You treated yourself to a trip to Shropshire, over the Easter holiday. This time you used your beard. You posed as a scout master looking for a suitable camping site for the summer, but what you really wanted was the lowdown on your family. You got it from Sir John Prout, but he isn't the simple old man you took him for. He has a retentive memory. He recognised your passport photograph the moment he saw it."

"Phooey!"

"Is that the best you can do?" demanded Beech smugly, "Try it on a judge and jury. After that, you went back to London and set to work. First of all an anonymous letter, then the break-in at James Winter's house and the planting of the arsenic. It worked like a charm. You should have left it at that. The old man couldn't have lasted long. But you couldn't wait. The shock of the murders hadn't finished him off, as, no doubt, you had hoped. But you hadn't much time. You had had to make arrangements for forwarding of letters, both for yourself and Ben Price. You used an accommodation address for both. And through that arrangement you had received a letter from Mr Walters, the lawyer, asking you to go to your grandfather at Astonley. You sent word to Ben in America that he must come home and to send a cable to Astonley, from the ship, on his way. That was a double safeguard and would place you nicely on the ship in case any inquisitive copper started asking questions. But it also meant that you had to leave the post office in order to show up at Astonley as your real self. So you handed in your notice. Only, you had another bright idea first. You would send off a telegram which might tip poor old Robert Winter out of this world into the next. I don't doubt that it gave you one hell of a kick to be interviewed by me over that telegram, in your capacity of counter clerk. You must have loved it."

"Is that all?" asked Tom, coolly insolent now, his anger under control.

"By no means. We come now to Arabella Manston. Ben Price couldn't keep away from women, could he? And this time he landed you in a jam. I expect he thought it a great joke to take her in and spin her a big tale about Astonley, until he had her just where he wanted her. In bed. He dodged her when they left the boat. It didn't matter to him if she went to Astonley. She would soon realise that she had been had. But he had reckoned without her determination. Somehow, she had got hold of the Bristol address. *Your* address. I imagine she went through his pockets while he was asleep. By all accounts, she was that sort of woman. She told a woman at her hotel in London that she thought she had been had, but that he wasn't going to get away with it. And she went away for an overnight trip. She didn't turn up at Astonley, so we reckoned that she must have gone to Bristol. Which she had. We found the hotel where she stayed, and your landlady gave her the Astonley address. So Mrs Manston went back to London well satisfied."

Beech paused, but this time Tom offered no comment.

"So," the Superintendent went on, "we reckon she wrote to you. And what do we find? A letter arriving here from Bristol. A letter which upset you very much."

"But that was about my poor old friend's death," Tom objected.

"Tell that to the Marines," Beech scoffed. "You never had a poor old friend. I suppose you never thought we would check up on this one. As it is, the time you were there, there wasn't a funeral in the whole of the Bristol area which could back up your story. Not of an old lady. I don't suppose that happens very often, not in a city that size. Just your bad luck. No, that letter was from Bella Manston, written from Bristol, and you went there, hoping to catch her. You summoned Ben to meet you there, too. I suppose he told you the whole miserable story. Of course, he knew where she was. She received a phone call in London that night. Which pleased her a lot. Meanwhile, you had laid your plans. You couldn't afford to let her set eyes on you, so she had to be killed. So you packed Ben off again, only this time to France. You engineered a quarrel with the family at Astonley, typed a letter to Mrs Manston, and took off in your car for Dover. There you kicked up a fuss so that they would remember you. Beech leant forward. "And they do remember you, beard and all. But you didn't go on the boat. Ben did."

Tom summoned up a mirthless laugh.

"And what did *I* do? Go on, I can't wait to hear."

"The following morning, Sunday, a bearded Australian gentleman hired a car in Dover. A dark blue saloon. He turned it in, in London, late on Monday night. The mileage he had done was enough to account for a trip to Oldchurch."

"Have you any idea," inquired Tom mildly, "how many Australians hire cars every day in this country?"

"Ah, but there was something special about this car. It

left its traces on a patch of mud on the old airfield outside Oldchurch. It was driven up here in the early hours this morning. And its tyres match exactly a set of tracks we found near Mrs Manston's body. So that disposed of Bella Manston. There's another point here. That airfield where she was killed has plenty of disused air-raid shelters. Ideal for hiding a body. Only she wasn't hidden. Therefore she was meant to be found. Why? Because the murderer had rigged up a jolly good alibi. And it so happens that you were the only person from Astonley who had one for that afternoon. There remained Ben Price. He would smell a rat once he heard what had happened to Bella. And he was a liability, with his weakness for women. So, on Tuesday morning, you crossed to Boulogne."

"How could I? According to you he had my passport."

Beech shrugged.

"There are ways and means. He met you at Boulogne, with your car. You drove outside the town and there you killed him, left him in a ditch, reassumed your own identity, and drove off."

Tom stood up.

"I've had enough of this. You may think yourself very clever, but you can't prove anything."

Beech stood up too.

"That's what you think?" he replied unpleasantly, "We've witnesses all over the place and more to come, once the French police have finished their investigations. Quite enough to take you in. Which I propose to do. Now."

Tom stared at him.

"My God! You mean it!" he exclaimed blankly.

"What do you think I've been doing?" roared Beech, "Reciting a poem?"

"Then why don't you finish the job and accuse me of poisoning Roderick too?"

"That's just like your nerve," Beech flung back at him.

"But don't think you can put me off that way. You had the best opportunity to slip a dose of cyanide in his whisky, then doctor your own glass and the decanter while you are yelling for help. Not to mention getting rid of the bottle while you were waiting for us to come."

"Try proving that," Tom challenged him, "And why should I want to finish off Roderick for goodness sake?"

It was the weak point, the unsolved problem. Morton watched Beech closely to see how he would take it.

But the Superintendent merely brushed it aside.

"I've enough without that, Winter. Your trouble is that you have underestimated us."

Morton was thinking: So that is the way it is going to be; Beech will nab all the credit while every scrap of the work was done by Liston and Warren and their boys. If it had been left to Beech they would still have been trailing Marion Loring.

Once a bastard, always a bastard.

Marion was crouched in a corner of the old summer house. No one had used it for years, and it was a dump for broken garden furniture and unwanted tennis racquets.

Now it was a refuge.

In spite of herself she wondered what was going on in the house. She had been glad to escape from the study, from the presence of Superintendent Beech.

He was after Tom now.

She was aware of an overwhelming sense of relief. And was ashamed. She should be helping Tom in some way, remembering her own experiences at the hands of the police. Instead. . . .

They hadn't caught up with David.

That was the whole point.

"Marion!"

David's voice.

"Marion! Where are you?"

She stood at the door of the summerhouse, her knees trembling. He saw her, came rapidly across the lawn.

"Have you heard?" he demanded.

"Heard what?"

"Tom's been arrested."

She stared.

"Arrested? Don't you mean taken in for questioning? There is a difference. As I know."

David shook his head.

"No. Arrested. Don't ask me the details. I know nothing. But they have taken him away. And they are searching the house. They have found something, too. In the loft over the garage."

"David, I thought it was you," she blurted.

She dared not look at him.

"Because of Astonley, I suppose?" he asked in a hard voice.

She nodded dumbly.

"And what are you going to do about it, Marion? Have you told the police?"

"No."

"Why not? It might save Tom."

She turned away, speechless, shaking her head. It was shameful, but it was true: Tom would have to take his chance; she would never betray David. And now he knew it.

He put his hands on her shoulders, forcing her round to face him. But she would not look at him.

"Marion," he said quietly, "I asked you to marry me. That offer is still open."

Her head came up.

"You don't have to buy my silence, David."

The hands on her shoulders were suddenly no longer gentle. David shook her roughly.

"My good idiot, I am not a murderer. I have never coveted Astonley. It never even occurred to me that I might inherit it. And most certainly I did not embark on a campaign of mass murder to get it. I am very touched that you were not going to tell your suspicions to the police, but the suspicions themselves I find highly unflattering. Understand?"

The relief was now so great that she felt her heart would burst.

"If the police have arrested Tom, you can be sure that they have sufficient evidence against him to make it stick," he added.

"What will happen to him?"

She could spare a thought for Tom now. It was difficult to imagine him a murderer.

"And to Astonley?" she went on.

"If he is found guilty at his trial he won't be allowed to succeed."

"And you are next in line."

David shook his head.

"We will have to wait and see. Poor Tom, I have reason to be grateful to him."

"For Astonley?"

His hold on her shoulders tightened again.

"I wasn't thinking of that. He did my job for me. He killed James."

Marion shivered.

"David, let me go. After James, you don't want me. It is very good of you to offer to marry me, but I can manage quite well on my own."

"What nonsense is this?" he exclaimed, "I want you to marry me because I love you."

"But what about Flora Ludlow?"

He laughed outright.

"So you know about that, do you? I made a fool of myself over her for more years than I like to count. But I've been over it for a long time. Now, Marion, will you or will you not marry me?"

"Oh, yes, oh, yes."

His arms went round her and she put up her face for his kiss, wondering how she could ever have thought there was any other man for her in the whole wide world.

Late in the afternoon, Alec Liston and Charles Warren walked into the police station in Oldchurch. Inspector Morton, almost swaying on his feet from fatigue, came to them.

"How is it going?" asked Liston.

"He's a tough nut," acknowledged Morton, "We've got plenty on him, but still not enough. We want to sew him up right and tight. We've found Ben Price's things, suit-case and wallet, up above the garage at Astonley, but Winter's shut his mouth and won't say a thing. He's shaken, though."

"We have a little more for you."

"Have you, Mr Liston? Come on. This way."

He brought them to Superintendent Beech, red-eyed and ferocious.

"Try it on him yourselves," he said, with a disgusted wave of his hand. It was an admission of near-defeat.

Tom glared at the newcomers in sullen silence.

Liston pulled up a chair and sat down in front of him.

"Ben Price stayed at a hotel in Quimper, Brittany. I've had a man over there making a few inquiries. He's just phoned through his report. Would you like to hear it?"

"Suit yourself."

Liston smiled.

"You will find it interesting, I promise you. First of all,

Ben received a cross-channel telephone call on Monday evening, as a result of which he packed his bag and cleared out of the hotel early on Tuesday morning, the day he was murdered. You made that call, I presume?"

Tom said nothing.

"But the really interesting thing," Liston went on, "is the information that Ben had found himself a girl-friend in the short time that he was there. And had a pretty good time with her, too. So much so that she is willing to swear to the scar which he had on his stomach. Of course, he was posing as you, but you haven't got a scar in an intimate place, have you? So I think we can prove which of you was using the passport. And, if we dig around a bit, I expect we shall be able to find a female in the States who can give the same sort of testimony. What a lad he was."

Tom remained silent, but beads of sweat stood out on his forehead.

"But to return to this girl in Quimper. Like Bella Manston, she didn't fancy being left high and dry. So she wrote a letter. Only, of course, it went to you, at Astonley. That must have been a nasty moment when you realised that Ben had been up to his tricks again. And it put you back on the spot. Worse, for Roderick had seen that letter. I imagine he teased you about it. But that is why he had to go, too, wasn't it?"

Tom's jaw dropped.

"How—?" he began and stopped.

"Marion was there. She overheard."

"Leave her out of this," said Tom violently.

Liston's look was almost compassionate.

"Yes, I fancy you really care for her. But you were landed with Ben's fancy women, and you daren't let them live. I understand the girl in Quimper has received a telegram telling her that you would be back with her soon. It doesn't need much imagination to guess what you had planned for her."

There was a moment's silence.

Then Tom dropped his head into his hands.

"Oh God!" he groaned, "Ben and his bloody women."